THE LONELIEST COTTAGE

ALASKAN HEARTS, BOOK 1

MELISSA STORM

Editor: Megan Harris
Proofreaders: Falcon Storm & Jasmine Bryner
Cover by Daqri Bernardo at Covers by Combs

Partridge & Pear Press
PO Box 72
Brighton, MI 48116

To Falcon:

Who first introduced me to the beauty of Alaska
Whose experiences as a handler served as the inspiration
for this series
And who opened my heart to the greatest of loves

ABOUT THIS BOOK

Lauren Dalton's world shattered the day her father died. It shattered again when she found a box of old keepsakes commemorating a life she'd never even known he lead.

Heartbroken but determined, she accepts a seasonal job in rural Alaska to look after an injured musher's dogs while searching for the truth about her father's hidden past. But her cantankerous new boss comes with dangerous secrets of his own.

When a fire ravages part of the property, all will be revealed —and four-thousand miles away from the only home she's ever known, Lauren will discover just how quickly everything can change.

AUTHOR'S NOTE

Hi,

I am not Melissa. I'm her husband, Falcon. I was so happy when Melissa told me that she wanted to write sled dogs into a series and I freely offered up my experiences as a junior musher to her story.

Remember being a child and running as far and fast as you could and feeling that sense of pure exhilaration? I'm jealous of sled dogs because that's what they get to do. They love what they do so much that in order to keep the sled in place before the race, you sometimes have to use two snow hooks and a tether. Even then, it's not always enough. There are steel pipes planted in concrete at the starting lines of most trails, and the pipes are bent from how excited the dogs are to start running. And when they start running, everything just melts away. It's you, the dogs, and the beautiful Alaskan landscape stretched out before you.

What you just read is fictional, but several of the scenes are very real. I spent some time helping a friend after school as a handler. I met the dozens of dogs the musher (who was also a pathologist by day) had. The team I got to work with was mostly named after the seven dwarves, and they were all white. The first time I crested the hill to look at the kennels, I saw a field of ghost dogs bouncing around, eager to go for a run.

And when I first went out with them, it wasn't on a sled. No, they were pulling an ATV in neutral. That's how I knew that everything I thought I knew about mushing was wrong, or at least way off. Mushing required a lot of physical energy from the musher as well as the dogs. On more than one occasion, I shed several layers of clothes after overdoing it running alongside the dogs as they ran uphill or started to tire. On other occasions, I was chilled through to my core, the wind biting through every layer of clothing.

But the one thing that sticks out in my mind: the feeling of being a part of God's Creation. Everywhere I looked was natural beauty as far as the eye could see, the sounds of the dogs as they joyously ran to their hearts' content. And somewhere out there was the heartbeat of the world, set in motion all those eons ago.

— MR. STORM

CHAPTER 1

THE CALL CAME IN WHILE LAUREN WAS AT WORK. HER EYES practically crossed as she tried to make sense of the never-ending spreadsheet before her. She'd never cared for numbers, but when you graduate with an English degree in the twenty-first century, you take whatever job you can get.

In her case, it was data processing for a large New York-based company that sold their data to other data centers, so together they could invade people's personal space with the kinds of ads that stalked you around the Internet with an uncanny ability to know where you'd been and what you might buy.

Personally, she hated it.

Which is why she was all too happy for the distraction of whatever waited on the other end of that call.

She took off her headphones and picked up her cell phone. "Hello?"

A man with a deep, unfamiliar voice greeted her. "Lauren Dalton?"

"Yeah," she confirmed, doing her best to sound friendly but busy, just in case this was a sales call. She didn't have the money to buy anything even if she wanted to, which is why she was here at this mind-numbing job trying to make a few bucks so she could one day maybe pursue what she really loved.

That is, once she figured out what that might be.

The man on the other end of the line took a long breath out. "I'm Officer Reed. Is this Lauren Dalton, daughter of Edward Dalton?"

Panic gripped at Lauren's heart. She clearly wouldn't like whatever this man had to say, so why on earth was he dragging it out? This moment needed to be over, and it needed to be over now.

"What happened to my father?" she whispered, hardly capable of pushing the words out.

"I'm sorry to inform you that your father was involved in a traffic collision and has passed away."

Lauren let out a loud hiccough of a sob, eliciting irritated stares from the neighboring cubicles.

"There was a deer. We think he died instantly. I know

this is a hard time for you, but when you can, you need to come claim his effects at the station."

Dead? How could her father be dead? She'd just been home for Christmas. He'd given her a scrapbooking kit and a shelf full of novels, and she'd given him a fancy new coffee maker. How could he enjoy his morning lattes if he were dead? How could they take their yearly spring break trip to Disney World if he was gone from this world? And what about in the future when she got married—who would walk her down the aisle then?

She needed to be sure. "Can I see him?" she asked, choking back another sob.

Her father had been the only family she had left. Her mother had died when Lauren was too little to have formed any lasting memories of her, and both her parents had been only children, just like she was.

It had always been Lauren and Dad against the world.

But now it would just be Lauren, all by herself, and the world made a mighty opponent when you had no one to face it with.

"If that's what you want." The officer rattled off the location of the morgue and waited as she wrote it down on a sticky note.

"I'll be right in," she told him and hung up quickly after he'd given her the address. She looked back at the wall of numbers on her computer screen. Is that what people became once they were no more, just a series of numbers and data, likes and dislikes, buyer profiles and click behavior?

The thought made her sick. It would be up to her to make sure Edward Dalton was remembered for the incredible man he'd been and not just as part of someone's marketing quota for the year.

She shut her computer down, gathered her things, and went to find her boss. When she couldn't find her in the office, she checked the conference room, where, sure enough, Joanna Brocklehurst was wooing a couple of well-groomed, bored-looking clients.

"Lauren!" her boss gasped as the employee barged into the room and demanded an audience. "My apologies," she murmured to the clients, rising to her feet to meet her wayward employee.

"I'm going home early today," Lauren said and turned to leave again before the door had even managed to swing shut.

Mrs. Brocklehurst chased her out into the hallway. "Excuse you, you can't just barge into a meeting like that, and you can't leave early on reports day. You have responsibilities." She emphasized the word reverently, as if nothing could be more important than her work for data corp.

"Yes, I have responsibilities and I need to go see to them. I'll be back on Monday, probably."

"Monday? But it's only Wednesday. I'm sorry, but I can't grant you time off with such short notice."

"Fine, then I won't be back. At all. I quit. Good luck with the reports."

Sure, it would have been easy enough to explain what had happened and why she needed to go, but somehow, she just couldn't bring herself to speak of her father in the past tense or to share any part of him with the stingy boss who signed subsistence level paychecks for her employees while vacationing at St. Bart's.

She'd given too much of herself to this place already. It was time to move on, to make something of the Dalton name, now that it would be entirely up to her to keep their legacy alive.

❄

LAUREN REACHED the morgue a couple hours later despite driving at least ten above the speed limit the entire time. Perhaps if she drove fast enough, she could turn back time like in those popular '80s movies with Michael J. Fox.

But instead of revisiting the happy past, she soon came face-to-face with her new future, and it wasn't one she wanted any part of.

The mortician had done a good job cleaning him up, but dark bruises still mottled her father's skin. Cuts and scrapes peppered his arms, though no blood—indeed, no sign of life at all—clung to them.

And when had he gotten so old?

She still thought of her father as the young man with brown hair and a few days' scruff framing sharp, green eyes she'd always wished she'd inherited instead of her dull browns. She thought of him as the man who'd graciously attended all her school Mother's Day events since he was her mom just as much as he'd been her dad. He was the man who'd changed her diapers, taught her to walk. He'd had to help her understand her first period, comforted her after her first heartbreak.

He'd been her world, and now—just like that—Lauren's world had ceased to turn.

The mortician beckoned her forward with a tight-lipped nod.

"Hi, Dad," Lauren managed to say as she stepped up to the gurney.

"I'm sorry for your loss," the other woman said, even though she had no idea, no idea at all, what had been lost to Lauren that day.

What kind of brave, new world would she face tomorrow? Because certainly Lauren would need to be brave to carry on in a world that no longer held her heart.

"I love you, Dad," she whispered, kissing her fingers and placing them to her father's impossibly cold cheek. She bowed her head and murmured a quick prayer. One day they would meet again, but Lauren still had many more days in which she'd need to make it on her own.

And make it she would, because that's how her father had raised her, and she refused to let him down.

CHAPTER 2

LAUREN DROVE TO HER FATHER'S HOME AND LET HERSELF IN with the key he kept stashed under a colorful frog garden ornament she'd painted for him in the third grade. The house felt as if it, too, felt the loss of its master, even though so few hours had passed since he'd last left it.

Coming home had often been her refuge after a stressful week at work or after yet another bad breakup. This time, she could scarcely recognize the house that had once served as the backdrop to all her most precious memories.

One thing in particular bothered her today, though. Why had her father been out driving that morning, and why so recklessly that he failed to see the deer dart across the expressway until it was too late for either of them?

As a retired school teacher, he didn't have anywhere pressing he needed to be. And when he did, he preferred to walk through their small town to greet his former students and the neighbors he'd known for years. So why had things been different today?

She'd need to plan a funeral, and no doubt half—if not, all—the town would be in attendance. And she would have to sort his things, settle his estate, make sure everything was buttoned up neatly with her father's life.

But what happened next?

She no longer had a job, and she knew she wouldn't be able to bear life in this place on her own. Despite loving her neighbors, she'd now become the one they would all pity and whisper about when she was nowhere to be seen. That's not how Lauren wanted to live. She wanted to live a big life, one that would honor her father's memory rather than linger in his shadow.

Lauren found the coffee maker she'd bought her father for Christmas just a couple weeks before and was happy to see he'd gotten the chance to use it. She set it to brew and went to her father's room to check for clues as to why he'd gone out that day.

It felt strange rummaging through his things when he'd so recently used them, almost like an invasion of privacy. But that was silly. She and her father hadn't kept any secrets from each other over the years. It's why their relationship had been so strong. He spoke candidly to her about her mother's death, about whether or not there was enough to pay the bills each month, about everything.

He'd prepared Lauren for life as best he knew how, which Lauren knew was far better than most young women her age. But he'd never taught her how to carry on without him. They'd both foolishly assumed that such a day would be a long way off, that Lauren would be married, with kids, living her best life—not a freshly unemployed nobody lacking any clear direction.

She returned to the kitchen and poured herself a mug of coffee. Normally she'd soften the taste with extra milk and sugar, but today she savored the sharp, acidic flavor as it hit her tongue. Carrying her mug with her, she returned to the bedroom and opened up the closet.

Her father's shirts hung in a straight row, neatly pressed and ready for wears that would never come. In the far corner, a stack of four shoe boxes pressed against the wall. It was where he kept his memory boxes. They'd often leaf through the contents together as he told Lauren stories of her mother and how much alike they'd been, how proud she would've been.

Proud of what, though? Lauren wondered with a sad, nostalgic sigh.

She pulled the boxes from the closet and set them on the neatly made bed. She knew the one with the turquoise lid held the memories and photos of her mother. The purple one contained Lauren's childhood, and the orange her high school years. She didn't remember a fourth box and now eyed the additional brown cardboard container with suspicion.

Naturally, she opened that one first.

Immediately she was met with neatly stacked newspaper clippings and old Polaroid photos. The Anchorage Daily News, the masthead on the first read. But hadn't they always lived in New York?

She continued to read the article:

Edward Dalton becomes the youngest musher to place in the top twenty at the Iditarod, beating out several more experienced men and securing his place as a rising star and a serious contender for next year.

Dog racing? Alaska? None of this made sense. Why had her father kept something so innocent from her all these years? And why had he stopped if he was one of the greats?

She continued to leaf through the contents of the box, unearthing pictures of dogs, tightly bundled men, and even an old collar. Clearly this had meant something vital to her father, but again, she could not figure out why he'd keep this, of all things, from her.

She took out her phone and did a search on "sled dogs." Perhaps there was some seedy underbelly she didn't know about? The idea seemed ridiculous, especially given how straight-laced her father had always been dating back as far as she could remember.

One of the top results on Google was for the country music star Lolly Winston. Lauren owned both of her CDs and liked to listen to Lolly on the long commute to her old job. Curious, she clicked into an article about the Sled Dog Rescue Organization, a charity founded by Lolly and her husband Oscar Rockwell roughly two years back.

"We need to preserve the last great race, and to make sure retired dogs find loving forever homes," Lolly had been quoted. "There's something so beautiful about seeing these dogs in their element both on the slopes and at home."

Lauren found herself nodding along as she read and, before she knew it, she'd clicked over to the SDRO website, which featured a list of adoptable dogs along with other ways to help.

If you have the heart, they need the home.

Lauren liked that, especially considering it felt like a heart was the only thing she had left these days—and a badly broken one at that.

The longer she stayed on the website, the more it called to her.

These dogs will love you with everything they've got. They are so grateful to be rescued, to get a second chance.

A second chance, Lauren thought. I wish someone would rescue me.

And then she found their blog, and at the top of the feed was a picture of a handsome, rugged-looking man standing with a group of nearly thirty dogs.

Shane Ramsey, the post said, has long been considered one of the top racers of the day. Unfortunately, an ill-fated training run with his snow machine has crushed in his kneecap. The injury will require a long and difficult healing process, if indeed healing is to occur at all. Although his condition is stable, no word yet as to whether he will be able to continue racing. Mr. Ramsey is now searching for a handler to help care for his team while he attempts to make a full recovery. All the other teams are already deep into this season's training, leaving Shane and his team sidelined. That is why he's come to us, and we are now coming to you. If you have the heart, we have a job and a home for at least the next three months, but for as long as a year. Will you help care for this incredible team? Please enquire at...

Lauren pressed the call button as soon as she recognized that a phone number had been given. The paper had called her father one of the top racers of his decade, and now the blog had said the same thing about this Shane guy. She no longer had a job, a home, anything.

It felt like everything was leading her to this one place, so she took a deep breath and stepped toward her calling.

CHAPTER 3

ABOUT A WEEK LATER, LAUREN FOUND HERSELF DRIVING HER temporary rental car up a long, lonely stretch of road. Snow walled her in on every side and the pure, clean sky merged perfectly with the thick powder on the ground.

It had taken her eight days of non-stop organizing to wrap things up in New York, and she was ready for this clean break from her life. As expected, her father's funeral had been well attended, and thanks to his intense commitment to keeping everything neat and tidy, readying the house for sale hadn't taken much, either.

He'd left her a neat bundle and a modest nest egg with which she could build something new for herself. She would be okay, but she wasn't quite sure as to the particulars yet.

An eagle soared into her view from above, and she wondered if it might be a good omen. Freedom. She hadn't realized she'd needed freeing from her life, but free she had become.

Might as well make the most of it.

As she drove farther and farther from Anchorage, she started to wonder whether she'd missed a turn off. But given that there were hardly any turn offs, twists, or anything other than straight, flat road, she couldn't see how that would be possible.

Finally, at last, when Lauren was certain she'd fall asleep at the wheel from the boring monotony of white, white, and more white, straight, straight, and more straight, she found an old, worn sign that proclaimed Puffin Ridge just ahead.

"Just" of course was relative, because after her turn she still needed to drive another half hour to find the address she'd scrawled onto a sticky note and slapped upon the dash.

1847 Thornfield Way loomed perfectly into view as she navigated her way down an icy incline and toward a homely looking cabin made of red cedar and situated amidst the clearing of a large pine forest.

Her brakes stuck as she attempted to slow, but luckily there was more than enough snow to pad her stop. Here it was, her new home for the next three to twelve months.

She applied a fresh coat of lip gloss and ran her hands through her chestnut hair, using the rearview mirror to check her appearance. Good enough, she decided and grabbed up her shoulder bag to head inside.

A middle-aged woman with gray liberally streaked through her strawberry blonde hair greeted Lauren at the door. Oh no, had she missed that turn after all? Was this the wrong house?

"You must be Lauren. Come inside before you catch your death," the woman said with big sweeping gestures as she ushered Lauren in.

"Hi, are you Shane's... wife?" The woman looked more of the age to be his mother, but Lauren didn't want to insult her when she may well be the only person around for miles.

The woman laughed heartily, and Lauren immediately liked her from that moment on. "Goodness no. I'm Mary Fairbanks. I'm the next closest thing to a neighbor Mr. Ramsey has, so I've been filling in while he was short of help. Speaking of, now that you're here, I best be off. I have a casserole in the oven back home."

Lauren found it odd that a woman at least a dozen years Shane's senior would be calling him Mr., but she was far more concerned about being left alone when she had no idea what was expected of her.

"Wait," she pleaded. "Is Shane here? Can you take me to him before you go?"

"Mr. Ramsey," Mary enunciated over the ruckus of barking that rose from outside. "And, no, he's gone to town for a doctor's appointment. It's just you and the dogs this afternoon. Why don't you go say hi? They're out back in the kennels, as I'm sure you guessed." She looped a thick home-knit scarf around her neck, then shrugged into her coat. "I really need to go, but we'll see each other again sometime soon. Nice to meet you, dear," she said as she reached for the door knob. She paused and looked back at Lauren as if forgetting something. "Oh, and good luck."

Lauren thought she heard the old woman murmur "you'll need it" as she stomped down the walk and out of view.

CHAPTER 4

LAUREN WATCHED MRS. FAIRBANKS UNTIL SHE DISAPPEARED over the horizon, leaving her alone in the strange, new place that would now be her home. The house was messily kept with stray papers cluttering many a surface and a basket of laundry crowding the narrow hallway.

Would this be her job now, too?

She was here for the dogs, no question, but wondered if perhaps the man might need her even more. Had she taken on more than she could handle?

No, life with Shane Ramsey and his merry team of huskies may prove to be a challenge yet, but at the very least it would be interesting—and at best, it might help her uncover secrets about her father's past.

And she would start by saying hello to her charges.

After fishing a knit cap from her bag, she headed out

back where several long rows of colorful, flat-topped dog houses sat in sharp contrast to the surrounding mountains of snow. As soon as they saw her, the dogs began to pull against their ties, some of them jumping up on top of their houses to gain a better vantage point.

Excited barks, whines, and howls reverberated across the valley. And Lauren knew then that she had made the right choice in coming here.

Carefully, she approached the cluster of kennels and introduced herself to the first dog, who eagerly leaped up to give her kisses on her cheeks.

One by one, Lauren made her way through the grid of houses, introducing herself to each dog in turn. Her eye was drawn to one dog in particular, a red husky who stood calmly at the edge of the pack, watching Lauren with a cautious eye.

"Aren't you a pretty one?" Lauren said, making her way over to the dog and kneeling to allow it to sniff her.

A glistening copper tag hung from the dog's collar.

"Briar Rose, huh?" Lauren said, scratching her new friend between the ears. "Well, that's a pretty name. And what about the rest of you?"

She turned, startled to find that she was not alone in the yard.

"I thought they were sending a professional, someone with experience," said a man she recognized from his pictures as her new employer, Shane Ramsey. He scowled as he watched her, clearly displeased with what he saw.

"And how do you know I haven't got any?" she demanded, rising to her full height but still standing at least a head beneath the stranger who stood supported by two thick wooden crutches.

"Every single thing about you shows you aren't cut out for this," he snarled.

"Can we start again, please?" She approached the gate and let herself out to stand with him in the path that had been cleared between the house and the kennels. Reaching out her gloved hand, she smiled and waited for him to accept her greeting.

"I'd rather not," he said, gathering up his crutches and turning back toward the house.

"Now wait just a minute!" Lauren cried. The sound of her voice cut sharply through the thin air, both alarming the man and exciting the dogs.

She watched as his posture stiffened and he slowly turned himself to face her once more. As he did, however, his left crutch caught a patch of ice, and soon he'd crumpled into the snow, cursing in pain.

"Let me help you up!"

"No, you've done quite enough already," he said. "Just hand me my crutch and leave me alone."

She picked up the walking aid and held it toward him.

When he reached for it, she jerked it away and said, "Not until you tell me why you're so rude."

He growled, making a sound not entirely human as he did. The effect, when combined with the growth on his face, gave him a feral appearance. "Because you aren't the kind of person I wanted to hire. But seeing as there weren't any other applicants, it seems I'm stuck."

"Then you should be grateful I'm here. Clearly you can't manage by yourself."

"I'm not sure having an inexperienced little girl here is much better."

"Don't talk to me like that."

He snorted and looked away.

"I mean it. I quit my job and moved a few thousand miles to be here. I may not have much experience, but I'm ready to learn. You need to treat me with respect."

"And if I don't?"

"Then know that I have no problem standing up to you, seeing as I'm the only one with two good legs around here." She stood as straight and tall as she could, and watched as his rigid posture softened in the snow.

Much to her surprise, that last comment drew out a smile from the otherwise sour-faced Shane. "Fine. Now can I have my crutch back, please?"

She handed it over and helped pull him to his feet. "There, now that wasn't so hard, was it?"

He walked away, muttering a string of curses under his breath. Lauren and the dogs watched in silence until Shane Ramsey had let himself back into the house and slammed the door shut behind him.

"Is he always like this?" she asked Briar Rose, slipping her fingers through the fence links to pat the dog's soft fur.

The dog didn't respond to the question, but Lauren was quite sure she could figure out this particular answer for herself.

CHAPTER 5

LAUREN SPENT THE NEXT HOUR IN THE COMPANY OF THE dogs. She read the names on their collars and matched them to each dog's unique markings and personality. Briar Rose had quickly become her favorite, even though she didn't seem to fit in well with the others—not just her calmer demeanor and slighter build, but also her name.

The other huskies and malamutes were named predictable plain things like Alice, Bob, Carol, Dennis, and so on. In fact, there was a name for each letter of the alphabet—and Briar Rose made twenty-seven total.

While all the dogs were happy to spend time with Lauren, Briar Rose was the one who stuck to her side for the whole of the hour. Lauren was very tempted to bring Briar into the house so she would have at least one friend inside, but she preferred to avoid added confrontation with Shane.

After all, it was very likely he'd consider her making a pet of his sled dog "unprofessional."

She settled for a quick goodbye and promise to see the dog again bright and early in the morning, then made her way inside to see about dinner.

Her employer had beaten her to it, though. Shane stood hunched over a boiling pot of water, struggling with a box of spaghetti as he tried to keep himself propped up on his crutches and away from the splash zone of the roiling water. He wore plaid pajama bottoms and a button-down shirt. His feet were bare, which seemed a mistake in this weather even with being indoors.

"Let me help with that," she offered, rushing across the small eat-in kitchen before she even had a chance to remove her coat or boots.

Shane jerked the box out of her reach, accidentally flinging half its contents to the floor. "Now look what you made me do!"

"I didn't make you do anything. That's all you and your stubbornness." She stooped down to pick up the scattered noodles, but Shane interrupted her again.

"If it's my mess, then I'll clean it up." She watched as he lowered himself to the ground, fresh pain evident in his features every inch of the way. And she allowed him to struggle on his own as she removed her winter gear and pulled her hair up into a high ponytail. During that time, he made hardly a dent at all in the cleaning.

"Why am I here?" she demanded, stooping down and forcing him to look her in the eye. "If you're going to insist on doing everything yourself, then why did you hire me?"

"I didn't hire you, the SDRO hired you for me," he reminded her with a muted grumble.

"Okay, fine, but regardless, I'm here to help. Can you just let me?" She glared at him still, but the hulking, muscular man refused to meet her gaze.

"If that's how you want it, then be my guest," he said, gesturing toward the remaining mess and almost losing his balance yet again in the process.

"First let me help you up," she said.

He groaned but submitted as she looped his arm over her shoulder and pulled him to his feet. Despite his injuries, Shane was still strong and able to bear the brunt of his own weight once Lauren helped him to regain his balance. That was good, seeing as he easily outweighed her by eighty pounds. They were a study in contrasts. Him a large, lumbering, and wild-looking man. Her a small, trim woman whose appearance was neatly kept and movements graceful.

Shane stiffened, bringing them both to a stop. "No, not to the chair. I need to finish making dinner," he argued.

"What's for dinner? Spaghetti? I think I can manage

that." She took him to the small kitchen table and sat him down before his mess of papers.

He said nothing as she finished cleaning the debris from the checker-tiled floor and then making their dinner with the noodles that hadn't already gone to waste. Placing a bowl of pasta marinara before him, she turned to go find solace in her room.

"Wait," Shane said without looking up.

"Yes?"

"Join me for dinner at least."

"Oh, so now you want to talk, do you?"

He shrugged and glanced at her for a brief moment, his ocean blue eyes clearly concealing secrets within their depths. "I want to learn about this stranger who will be living in my house, yes."

"Okay then." Lauren prepared a bowl for herself and sat opposite of him, nudging some papers out of the way to avoid turning them into impromptu placemats. "So what do you want to know?"

He put his fork down and stared at her head on. His eyes were unabashed in sharing their assessment—he didn't trust her, not yet. "I want to know why you're here," he said.

"To help you. We've been over that."

"But why? The organization said you were from New York, and we've also already been over the fact that you have no experience, so let me ask again: Why are you here?"

Well, if he didn't trust her, then she didn't trust him either. Why else would he be so naturally suspicious of her unless he had something to hide? With any luck, she could stay just long enough to help the dogs, uncover the mystery about her father's past, and figure out what she wanted to do next. Then she could cut her losses with the grumpy Mr. Shane Ramsey and leave him far, far behind.

She met his eyes, refusing to blink or look away. "I'm here to do a job. That's all you need to know."

"I see. So that's how you want it." He smiled to himself, picked up his fork, and returned his attention to eating.

"That seems to be how you want it, and I'm happy to comply." She raised her fork too, a challenge—she would take whatever he had to throw at her, but she wouldn't take it sitting down.

"Very well," he said.

"Very well." They finished their meal in silence and then went their separate ways for the remainder of the evening.

CHAPTER 6

By the time night rolled around, Lauren found herself exhausted from the long day of travel, meeting the dogs, and from her run-ins with Shane Ramsey. She found her bedroom easily enough. It was the one with her name plastered on the door, much like the dogs' names were displayed on placards atop each of their bright little houses.

Inside she found a simple twin bed with a flannel set of sheets, which matched Shane's pajamas almost perfectly. A stack of blankets lay neatly at the foot of the bed. In fact, everything about this room was neat, tidy, and sterile. It didn't match the rest of the house at all. The walls were white, and the wood of the bed frame and matching dresser were light pine. Even the carpet was a soft beige, which had somehow managed to remain stain free despite its light color.

Lauren retrieved her luggage and went about making the room a tad more lived in. She started by unpacking a framed photo of her and her father from this past Christmas and setting it up neatly on her nightstand. There she found a stack of papers held together with a red paperclip.

It said House Rules at the top in huge bold font.

She rolled her eyes and turned the page where a lengthy bulleted list followed a short introductory paragraph:

Lauren Dalton, hereafter called The Handler, will abide by the following rules while she is living in residence at the home and place of business of one Shane Ramsey, hereafter referred to as The Employer.

Lauren rolled her eyes again and let out a long sigh. If this kept up, she'd find herself permanently scarred from the whole ridiculous experience. She drew her eyes back to the page and continued reading:

PART I.

Section 1. The Handler shall sleep and spend her leisure time in the white room. She may have free rein of the house—excepting the areas outlined in Section 2—provided she does not intrude on the privacy or comfort of The Employer.

Section 2. The Handler is not allowed to enter either the master bedroom or the outside shed under any circumstances. These areas are for The Employer alone.

PART II.

Section 1. The Handler is expected to prepare two nutritionally balanced meals per day for both herself and The Employer as well as for the dogs.

Section 2. The Handler will run the dogs daily by taking them out one at a time and sticking to the marked path along the property, unless otherwise instructed by The Employer.

Section 3. The Handler must keep up all property and assets in accordance with...

And so it went for another three equally boring pages. At least she assumed they'd be boring. She just didn't have the patience to read Shane's ridiculous rules any farther. This was going to be a long stay, even if she managed to get out of there before the three months were up. Lauren skimmed the thing, found a place to sign and date, and then returned it to the kitchen table as instructed.

Afterward, she changed into her own pajamas, which were thankfully not flannel like the rest of her bedding, and tucked into bed with her eReader. She'd started a new book on the flight up and only had a few chapters left until she could find out how it ended.

Reading could keep her company, even if "The Employer" could not. She would get by. One way or another, she would be fine.

But why couldn't she put Shane Ramsey out of her mind? Why did she continue to turn the mystery of his odd behavior over in her mind again and again? It would likely continue to bother her until she could figure out why he was so stern and why he had instantly disliked her. If she couldn't change his mind about her, maybe she'd be able to change her mind about him by learning whatever truth motivated his strange actions.

Yes, it was going to be a long stay, but maybe she could find a way to make it fly by a little faster. Resolved to unravel not only the secrets of her family but also of her new employer, Lauren soon fell asleep without getting the chance to finish her novel.

CHAPTER 7

THE NEXT MORNING, LAUREN AWOKE TO THE SOUND OF twenty-seven dogs barking at the rising sun. She squinted through half-veiled eyelids, taking a moment to remember where she was and why.

A pounding sounded on the wall, followed by Shane's muffled growl, "Go feed the dogs!"

"Go feed the dogs," she mimicked, a part of her hoping the old grump had heard as she dressed for the outside.

The dogs were just as eager to see her today as they had been yesterday. They pulled against their leads, hopped on top of their houses, and ran energetic circles around their kennels.

"Good morning, lovelies!" she sang, going through and giving each dog a pat on its head as she reminded herself of their names.

Briar Rose greeted her the most warmly of all, actually letting out a low, pathetic whine when Lauren continued on to say hello to the next dog.

"Aww, Briar. I'll take you out first. I promise. But first, how about some breakfast?"

Apparently, that was the right thing to ask, because the team's excitement reached a fever pitch as Lauren headed off in search of the dog food. Noting the old wooden shed round the side of the house, Lauren headed there first. It was bolted up tight, and its windows were obscured with cardboard. So this must be the shed mentioned in Shane's ridiculous house rules, one of the two places Lauren was not allowed to go.

This realization made her tug at the door handle with even more force, but it wouldn't budge. What was in there that was so private? She wanted to spend more time trying to figure that out, but the dogs were manic with excitement now, and if she didn't feed them soon, Shane would no doubt come out to see about the holdup—and such an exchange would not be pleasant, especially first thing in the morning.

At last she found the dog's kibble in the garage, along with a hose she could use to fill up their water dishes. When she rejoined them at the kennels, she noticed that each only had a single bowl instead of the two they needed, so she dumped the food on the ground and filled the bowls to the brim with water, which froze over almost immediately in the frigid climate.

"What am I doing wrong?" Lauren asked Briar Rose, who sadly didn't have an answer for her.

Once the red husky had finished her meal, Lauren unhooked her from the kennel and took her for a walk around the property. Briar stayed tucked in at Lauren's heels as they tromped through the snow. Was she really going to have to do this with twenty-seven dogs, one at a time, every single day she was here?

She let Briar off the leash so the old dog could run and really stretch her legs, then returned to the kennels to see about grabbing a couple more dogs to exercise.

Shane was there, kicking at one of the water dishes and mumbling under his breath. Briar Rose ran right over to him and jumped up to plant a series of enthusiastic kisses on his face.

"What's going on here?" Shane said, turning toward Lauren with a deep scowl on his face.

"I fed the dogs and now I'm walking them, one by one like your rules dictate." She had half a mind to add "sir" but didn't want to make him even angrier than he already was, no matter how amusing that might be.

"Why is there ice in the bowls? Didn't you follow my instructions about the slurry?"

"Slurry?" She giggled at the funny word. "Is that one of those Inuit words for snow?"

Shane let out a deep sigh. "You're going to be more trouble than you're worth. You know that?"

"Maybe if you taught me how you wanted things done, you wouldn't be so disappointed all the time," she pointed out, but he ignored her snide remark and jumped into enraged lecture mode.

"Step one: give the dogs slurry—warm water and food in one dish to keep it from freezing over." He kicked at the bowl again. "Step two: keep the dogs on leash, always. No free running unless you want them to fight. Step three: you'll preserve your energy better and use theirs up more if you get on the small sled. Step four—"

"Hold on a sec. You're giving me a lot of information all at once and I don't have anything to write it down with."

He sighed again and pinched the bridge of his nose with thickly gloved fingers. "That's why I wrote it down for you. You didn't read the rules before signing, did you?"

She hesitated, which apparently gave him all the answer he needed.

"I thought you said you take this job seriously."

"I do. I just didn't realize there would be no on-the-job training and that you would be so particular about how everything is done. They're just dogs, Shane. Dogs need love more than anything."

"You have got to be kidding me? Love?" He actually had the audacity to laugh at her now. "And they are not just dogs. They are my entire livelihood. They're champion racers who need to stay in shape. They were born to run, and just because I can barely walk doesn't mean they should be tied up all season. So forget the love and focus on your duties. Once you make sure all the important things are handled each day, you have my blessing to use whatever energy you have left—if you have any at all—to shower the puppy wuppies with wuv."

She raised an eyebrow at him, but he didn't seem to notice. "Are you making fun of me?"

"Just stating the obvious. It's not my fault you have no idea what you're doing, and it's also not my fault you didn't read the rules." He cleared his throat and glanced at her for a moment before heading back toward the house and calling over his shoulder, "Now put that dog back on her lead and do the job right."

Lauren knew then that Shane's friendship would not be easily won. As much as she challenged him, he would challenge her right back. She knew what she was fighting for—a fresh start for her future and illumination of her father's past —but what on earth was Shane working so hard to keep hidden?

CHAPTER 8

LAUREN HOOKED THE DOGS UP TO THE SLED ONE BY ONE AND ran them as Shane had instructed. Even though she was exhausted after a few hours, her team didn't seem any less energetic than usual.

Committed to going back out after a quick lunch, she headed inside to see what was left in the scant pantry.

Shane sat by the window in his big recliner. Apparently he'd been watching her. For how long, she had no idea—but the realization made her uncomfortable.

"Were you spying on me?" she asked, trying to sound more light-hearted than she felt.

He rubbed his palms on his pajama pants and sat up a bit straighter in his chair. As if he needed any added help to intimidate her. "Spying? No. It's my job to watch you and make sure my dogs are safe and being well taken care of."

"It would be easier if you taught me what to do," she pointed out yet again.

He smiled as if he enjoyed their nearly constant battles. "You're supposed to already know what to do."

So they'd reached this impasse. Again. Lauren rolled her eyes and headed back to the kitchen.

"Where are you going?" he called after her. His chair creaked as he let down the foot rest.

"To see about lunch. You hungry?"

"Yes, but I'm not sure we have much of anything here. When are you going to the store?"

"After I finish exercising the dogs, I guess." She dug into the very back of the pantry and found some boxed goods that may or may not have expired. "How were you living before I came here? It seems that nothing is taken care of and hasn't been for a long time."

He shrugged. "I'll grab an apple or something after my shower."

"Good, you need a shower. You stink." He didn't really, but she wanted to get in another jab while she could, and the set up was far too easy. Why did she enjoy bugging him so much? Did he enjoy vexing her, too?

He held her eyes for a few seconds, a challenge, then burst into a smile. "Tell me that again after you actually break your first sweat working the dogs. By the way, they'll tire faster if you add some weights to the sled." He appraised her, looking her up and down, then added, "You're too small to offer much resistance."

Lauren bit back a reminder that this information would have been more helpful before she'd spent half her day trying to exercise the dogs and returned her attention to finding something—anything—to eat. How she wished she would have hung onto her rental car for a few extra days, so she could easily pop into town and get some groceries. As hungry as she was though, she didn't feel quite ready to ask a favor of Shane, especially one as big as borrowing his car.

"Well?" Shane asked, hobbling into the kitchen behind her.

"Well what?" she grumbled. "Go take your shower, stinky."

"If you have half the heart that you do a mouth, you'll win the dogs over in no time."

She wondered if that was his way of telling her that he liked her—and if it even mattered to her whether or not he did. "Good to know," she said plainly. "Now please go away."

He scoffed, but did as told.

As Lauren fished some peanut butter and graham crackers from the nearly bare pantry, she wondered more about her employer and how he had come to be like he was. Shane Ramsey had real moments of humanness—whenever he cracked a smile or teased her or let any part of himself shine through his gruff exterior.

Mostly, though, he was a beast of a man. Hardly even a man at all.

Luckily for her, Lauren wasn't afraid of monsters. And she would figure out Shane's deal sooner rather than later. She'd always been too curious to let a good mystery go unsolved, and now she had two of them.

First, she'd learn about why her father had given up racing, why he'd kept it from her, and what he had been doing on the day he died.

Then she'd find out what horrible thing life had done to turn Shane Ramsey into his current beastly incarnation. Perhaps there was a better version of him buried somewhere deep within.

CHAPTER 9

As Lauren stood contemplating the expiration date on a jar of strawberry jam she found nestled in the back of the fridge, the front door to the cabin opened, admitting a red-haired woman bundled tightly against the cold. She watched as the stranger carefully removed her outerwear and set it neatly in the closet.

"Can I help you?" Lauren asked, having decided against taking a chance on the jam and tossing it into the garbage beneath the sink.

The woman jumped slightly, but recognition soon shone within her light brown eyes. "Oh, you must be the new handler. Hi, I'm Grace Pearson." She rushed forward to offer her hand to Lauren, but Lauren remained cautious.

"Shane didn't mention a Grace. Can you tell me a bit more about why you're here?"

"He wouldn't, would he? He never mentions much of anything at all. Actually, I don't know your name yet, either." She paused.

"Oh, yeah. I'm Lauren."

"Hello, Lauren the handler. I'm Grace, Mr. Ramsey's physical therapist. I come by a few times per week to help work his legs and strengthen his back. You'll be seeing lots of me, I'm afraid."

Lauren brightened. She'd have a friend in this place after all. "What's to be afraid of? I'll be happy for someone to talk to other than Mr. Grump."

Both women laughed and took a seat at the small kitchen table. Lauren offered Grace some peanut butter and graham crackers, but she declined.

"Mr. Grump is definitely accurate now, but he wasn't like that before. Such a shame what happened to him."

"You mean the accident?" Lauren asked, wondering if this particular mystery might be solved more simply that she'd originally thought.

"That too, of course. But…" She frowned and, having apparently changed her mind, reached for the box of graham crackers. She took one long cracker from the package and broke it into quarters. "No, it's not my place to say." She shook her head back and forth longer than was natural for the gesture. "He doesn't talk about things for a reason, and I don't want to betray his confidence by blabbing on about things that aren't any of my business."

"But don't I have a right to know? I mean, seeing as I'm here living with him? If I'm playing house with a madman, I kind of need to know."

"Mad?" She resumed the long, slow shaking of her head, then dropped her voice to a whisper. "No, nothing like that. Hurting is more like it. But—"

The two women were interrupted by the arrival of their mutual employer, his sandy hair wet and brushed back neatly from his shower. He'd even shaved, revealing a strong jawline and flawless skin, both of which had previously been hidden by his raggedy beard. He looked nice—at least physically. His expression, though, was far from nice. "That's enough gossip for today," he boomed.

"So sorry, Mr. Ramsey. I wasn't going to say a word about any of it." Grace ducked her head in apology.

Shane turned fully toward Grace so that his back was to Lauren, effectively shutting her off from the continuing conversation. "My right knee has really been acting up this morning. Can we work it extra today?"

"Whatever you think is best. We'll get those kinks worked out for you," Grace said, ever the sycophant. Was she that way because she liked Shane or because she feared him? Maybe it was a bit of both, Lauren decided, as she slathered another cracker with peanut butter and shoved it in her mouth. When she'd had her fill of the cardboard-like lunch, she got up to go back outside with the dogs.

"Where are you going?" Shane asked, acknowledging her for the first time since he'd returned from his shower.

"Back to work," she said with a full mouth. A few crumbs escaped and fell onto her shirt.

"No," he said, watching as the crumbs settled on her breast. "Take my car and head into town. Find something decent for us to eat for dinner tonight."

"What about the dogs?"

"They'll make do. Tomorrow you'll exercise them correctly right from the start of the day. Today has already gone to waste anyway, so go do something useful while the sun's still up."

Lauren left with one look back toward Shane and Grace, who were setting themselves up on the floor of the living room. Grace was a good-looking woman, and she seemed to do whatever Shane asked of her. Soon her hands would be all over Shane as she helped him work out the kinks, and Shane had sent Lauren out so they'd be alone...

Given all this, Lauren wondered if Grace was just Shane's physical therapist or something more. More than that, though, she wondered why the sharp pang of jealousy gnawed at her gut.

Shane was horrible—the worst!—so why did she find herself increasingly drawn to him?

CHAPTER 10

THE COMMERCIAL AREA OF PUFFIN RIDGE SEEMED SMALLER than the valley property on which Shane's cabin and kennels were housed. In fact, it probably was.

A few blocks going north to south, and just two going east to west, made up the entire downtown area. Lauren quickly found the grocery store, seeing as it was by far the largest building in town.

As she parked, a few passersby stopped to wait for her, both inside cars and on foot.

"Are you Ramsey's new handler?" a middle-aged man wearing a thick cap with long ear flaps asked the moment she had exited the borrowed car.

She offered her best smile, happy to find out that not all of Alaska's residents were as cold as cantankerous Shane. "Yes, I'm Lauren."

"Not from around here, are you?" the woman at his side said in a way that hardly sounded like a question. Lauren assumed this was his wife, and a moment later, they locked hands, confirming her suspicion.

Lauren shook her head. "I'm from New York."

"Oh, we went there once. Busy place," the old man said, and his partner nodded.

"And how's Shane Ramsey? He treating you right?" the woman asked, her eyebrow raised sharply like a question mark.

"As good as to be expected, I guess," Lauren answered with a dismissive laugh.

The man and woman laughed, too, and another young woman pushing a cart with a toddler in the basket came over to join them.

"He's a bit of a local legend around here," the young mom whispered, as if she were afraid that Shane himself might overhear.

"For his bad temper?" Lauren asked, only half kidding.

"He wasn't always like that, you know."

"So I hear…" Would this be how she finally learned his secrets, in casual conversation with a few friendly locals?

"Heck, if I were him, I'd be angry at the world, too," the man said.

"There's no reason to be as cranky as Shane Ramsey," Lauren said.

"Oh, I wouldn't be too sure about that, darlin'. Did you know that he was expected to win the big race this year? The biggest of the big, the Iditarod. Each year he's been climbing the ranks, and this was supposed to be the one he finally took home. Except he had his accident almost as soon as the season started."

The women nodded, and one said, "Yes, he went from the top of his game to possibly being out of it all together. The way I hear it, he may never race again."

"Until next year, right?"

"No, not ever. His injury is pretty serious, you know? I don't know all the particulars, but they say he's lucky he can walk at all. Should've wound up in a chair with the way that snow machine flipped right on top of him and crushed in his knees."

Lauren winced as she pictured Shane in that deadly accident, but the man she knew wasn't a quitter. "He's working hard to get better. I'm sure he'll be fine in no time and back to working out his aggression on the trails."

"I hope you're right about that," the older woman said.

"It was nice to meet you," the woman with the toddler added with another sweet smile. "If you ever need anything, just stop by town. There's always someone around who can help."

The man nodded, causing the flaps on his hat to bounce back and forth. "You'll find that Puffin Ridge doesn't have many people, but the ones who are here are mighty friendly."

"I see that," Lauren said. "Well, I better get inside before I lose all feeling in my toes."

The three locals looked down at her boots. "Stop by Lowood's when you're through here and get yourself some proper winter attire. You'll need it," the older of the two women said, and they all nodded in agreement.

"I will. Thank you." She shook each of their hands and headed toward the door, wondering how long it might take for the feeling to return to her extremities. She bundled up tightly when she was outside with the dogs, but hadn't thought it would be necessary for a quick trip into town.

Quick, of course, was relative.

Lauren met two new acquaintances on the way to the entry, and several more as she made her way through the grocery store. Everyone was eager to introduce themselves and comment on the tragedy that was her employer. After a while, she began to nod along and pretend she knew what they were talking about. It was easier than admitting that she was living with a man she knew very little about.

If her father were alive, what would he think? Would he be angry at Lauren for putting her entire life on hold to follow what seemed a lot like a random whim? Or would he be proud she was following in his footsteps here?

She couldn't say for sure, so she decided to believe the

latter. Every day spent working with the dogs in Alaska brought her closer to the secret life her father had lived when he'd been about her age.

This place was in her blood, and her body seemed to know it, acclimating more quickly than she would have expected to the cold, the work, all of it. Regardless of Shane's temper and cold disposition, she knew this was the place she needed to be.

And it was up to her to make these months enjoyable.

Before heading home with her trunk full of groceries and overfilled bag of new winter wear items, she stopped off at the small florist shop that sat at the far corner of town.

"Hello! You must be the new handler everyone is talking about," the lady behind the counter greeted her. "Are you here for some meats?"

"Meats? Isn't this the flower shop?"

"Ahh, yes, that too. The flowers are more of a hobby. The sausages and game pay the bills, though. Happy to help you with either or both."

"I'm looking for a nice bouquet to brighten up my house. Umm, well, the place I'm living, at least."

The woman nodded and shuffled over to a cooler that held both floral arrangements and an assortment of smoked meats. "I don't have much in right now, just enough to keep stocked through folks' anniversaries, birthdays, and random acts of romance. I'll have more in a few weeks, though. Valentine's Day is the one time of year that the flowers here outnumber the meats."

"Do you have roses?" Lauren asked. She'd never been much of one for flowers, and roses were one of the few types of blooms she could name. Besides, it seemed more likely the tiny florist-slash-butcher would have roses than lilies, tulips, or daffodils.

"Why, I sure do!" the woman whipped out a bouquet of slightly wilted red roses with a dramatic flourish. "You know, roses used to be Mr. Ramsey's favorite. He'd often stop in and pick up a bouquet as he passed through town. Been a long time since I've seen him back, though."

"Perfect. How much?" Lauren asked, reaching into her pocket. Shane had given her money for the groceries, but she knew better than to use his credit cards to purchase a luxury item like this, regardless of what the old woman said. Luckily, she had enough left over from her last paycheck with data corp to cover this expense herself.

"Tell you what," the woman said with a huge smile as she wrapped up the bouquet. "You buy some of the elk jerky Mr. Ramsey likes so much, and I'll include the flowers for free. Think of them as a welcome to Puffin Ridge gift."

"Wow, thank you so much. You've got a deal."

A few minutes later, Lauren was back in her car full of

groceries with the fresh floral arrangement sitting on the passenger seat beside her. Soon she'd be back at the cabin on Thornfield Way, a place she was now beginning to think of as home.

CHAPTER 11

WHEN LAUREN RETURNED TO THE CABIN, SHANE WAS STILL exercising in the living room with Grace's help. Three times per week for more than two hours per session seemed like a lot, but Lauren wasn't an expert when it came to these things.

She left them to their task and quietly unloaded the groceries, pleased to find that they almost filled the once empty pantry. Unable to find a proper vase, she arranged the roses in a tall glass tumbler and set them in the middle of the table amidst Shane's mess of papers. Well, at least the pop of red helped to brighten the mess up a bit.

And as much as she'd like flowers to be a regular fixture at their table, she'd seen the prices attached to each bouquet, and they were more than double what she would have paid back in New York. That meant they probably had to be shipped from far, far away, especially during this season. Lauren had never been much of an environmentalist, but even she knew that was a huge load to add to her carbon footprint.

She quickly checked in on Shane and Grace again and, seeing that they were focused on their work, she decided to return to hers outside. She'd purchased the dogs some special treats to apologize for the mistakes she'd made earlier that day—and also just because spoiling them was fun. There was no rule that said working dogs couldn't also be well-loved dogs. At least she didn't think there was. She had, after all, failed to read Shane's ridiculous house rules in their entirety.

One by one, she visited each dog and gave out the special rawhide treats she had purchased for them. Then she headed toward the garage to find the sled weights Shane had told her about. As she passed the old wooden shed, she contemplated trying once more to pry it open, but she knew what a mistake that would be during broad daylight, and while Shane was home, no less.

Maybe she could read up on lock-picking later that night and give it a try whenever Shane left the house next—if he ever left. Because whatever was hidden inside that old wooden structure would undoubtedly shed light onto the secret of Shane, a mystery she was dying to solve.

A strangled cry shot across the valley, and Lauren raced

back to the kennels where two of the dogs had gotten into a fight over the rawhides. Even though they had all been tied back up, the large Malamute named Fred had managed to pull himself free and was now quarreling over who had the right to the treat Lauren had given to the much smaller husky, Georgina.

"Stop, stop!" Lauren cried, sprinting the rest of the way to the dogs.

Grace ran out of the house, too. "What happened?" she asked, but then looked down and saw for herself.

"I just wanted to do something nice for them," Lauren explained. "I figured if I got one for each of them, everything would be fine."

Grace grabbed Fred by the harness and dragged him and his house back over to the spot they belonged. The slight woman was far stronger than she appeared, and Lauren couldn't help but watch as she took care of everything.

"Do me a favor," Grace said, tossing the rawhide in the trash before returning to Lauren's side. "You don't tell him, and I won't either."

"But what did I do wrong?"

"These aren't normal dogs. They were bred to compete, and that's what they live for. You keep treating them like pets and they could get hurt or, worse, dead. You want to do something nice for them, then work them hard. Keep them running as fast and as long as you can. That's what Mr.

Ramsey hired you to do, and as long as he's still willing to fight to get better, that's what you owe it to him and these dogs to do. What happens after that, I can't say."

"I don't understand," Lauren said with a sigh. "But I'll do what you say. The last thing I want to do is cause anyone trouble, especially these sweet dogs."

Grace nodded. "Good. That's for the best. And I'll tell Shane that a coyote ran across the yard and got the dogs riled up. If there are any of those treats left over, find them and toss them in the trash to prevent any more fights. And, for the love of all that is holy, make sure you tie them up properly next time."

Lauren nodded as Grace returned inside for a few minutes, then came back out with her therapy equipment packed up and at her side. How was it that everyone understood how to do Lauren's job better than her? It seemed the more she tried, the worse she messed up.

She wanted to do work she could be proud of, work that would have made her father proud, and work that would ease whatever pain Shane Ramsey was trying to keep buckled up and close to the vest. Would she ever get it right?

CHAPTER 12

Lauren watched as Grace got in her car and drove off. She then ventured inside to make the hearty beef stew she'd planned for that night's dinner, hoping that Shane would be relaxed after his long afternoon of physical therapy.

She found him standing by the window, staring sightlessly into the yard. He turned toward her then, and his eyes immediately darted toward the floor where a mess of broken glass and scattered roses lay.

"Oh gosh! Let me help get this cleaned up," she cried as she grabbed a wad of paper towels from the counter and stooped down to assist with the mess.

"No," Shane answered forcefully. His hands shook with a tremor she hadn't seen before, but he made no motion to stoop down and clean up the flowers himself.

"Don't be silly," she said. "I'm here and able, and I think the flowers can still be saved. The glass, not so much." Lauren let out a small laugh. Accidents happened, and this one proved Shane was just as human as the rest of the world.

"No. Stop!" he said, suddenly enraged or frightened—she couldn't tell which. He kicked at the fragments of glass using his bare feet, and predictably opened a wound right on his sole. Blood mixed with water in a swirling, mesmerizing stream, like paint washing off from a brush.

"What are you doing? Are you crazy?" Lauren scolded. "Sit down and I'll go find a first aid kit."

"No, don't," he said again, but his voice had lost much of its power.

"Yes," she shot back. "Put that butt in the chair and hold this to your foot until I come back with some bandages." She tore a fresh wad of paper towels from the roll and shoved it into his chest, then rushed toward the bathroom.

It seemed she was always rushing these days. Some relaxing break this was!

Luckily, it didn't take her long to find a box of Band-Aids and some antiseptic ointment in the medicine cabinet. Even still, when she returned to the kitchen, Shane was not where she'd left him.

The door slammed, drawing her eye over to where he stood before a thin trail of blood. His shaking hands now bore fresh cuts as well.

"What is your problem?" Lauren screamed. This guy had zero self-preservation instinct, and she really didn't want him to die on her watch. She joined him at the door and pulled him back to the table.

A quick peek out the window confirmed that he had tossed the roses into the frigid yard. Why he would go out of his way to do that, she hadn't a clue.

"Now sit," she hissed, putting her hands on her hips as she waited.

"I told you not to worry about it," he said glumly. "I had it."

Lauren grabbed Shane's hand and inspected the tiny cuts and gashes speckled across his palm. "What was the rush? Why couldn't you have waited five seconds for me to grab the broom?"

He said nothing, but the shaking started up again.

"Fine, don't tell me." She sighed. "But whatever the reason for your outburst, we still need to get you patched up."

"What's the use?" he moaned. "You think this hurts? It's nothing compared to having a thousand pounds of metal bust in both your knee caps, pinning you in a huge snow drift where you're left for close to an hour to wonder if this is it, if this is how you'll die."

"That was incredibly specific. Did it happen to somebody we know?" Lauren dabbed some antiseptic onto a cotton ball and pressed it to the first of Shane's cut. He winced, but didn't cry out.

"But, small as this might be by comparison," she continued, "it could still get infected. And not liking how a few flowers looked on the table is no reason to risk that."

"It's not that..." Shane argued before losing heart and trailing off into silence.

She waited for him to say more, but he didn't.

"Well, whatever it is, what you did sure was stupid. It's a good thing I do all the work around here, because you're going to be even more useless with that gash on your foot and your hands cut to pieces."

"Why do you talk to me like that?" he asked, staring at his hands as she worked on them.

"Because that's the way you need to be talked to. I asked to start over that very first day, and you refused, so this is how our relationship is now, unapologetic and straight to the point."

Just as quickly as the corners of his face stretched in a grin, they fell back into his perpetual frown. "Maybe that's for the best."

Lauren turned his hand over and continued to work on cleaning up the cuts he'd sustained from frantically collecting the roses. "Maybe," she agreed. "But make no mistake about it: I'm going to figure you out eventually."

"So much confidence," he observed. "I doubt you'll be

able to do something that even I haven't managed to do myself, but good luck."

She had a feeling he really meant that, that he wanted to be figured out, if not by himself, then at least by somebody out there.

Seeing as he was softening more and more with each moment they spent together that evening, she decided to try again for some kind of explanation. "Will you tell me what you have against roses, especially considering you named one of your dogs Briar Rose?"

"Briar Rose is not my dog," he said pointedly, as if Lauren had made a terrible accusation without knowing it.

"Funny, seeing as she lives here in the kennels with your dogs."

"I keep her, but she's not mine."

"And the flowers?" She kept her face down as she worked, doing her best not to show how interested she'd become in finding out the answers to the many questions she found herself asking about why Shane was Shane.

"Are unnecessary," he finished for her before reverting back to his normal callous demeanor. "I don't like change, and I don't like you messing things up here."

"Well, excuse me for trying to add a bit of cheer."

"Who said I like cheer? Who said this place needed it?"

"Okay, Mr. Grump, you're done," she said, slapping the last of the bandages on his hands. "Now show me that foot."

"Careful of that glass," he said as she stooped down to inspect his sole.

She couldn't help but laugh. "Why should I be when you weren't?"

He smiled again, but then forced a cough to cover it up. This time when she applied the antiseptic to his gash, he jerked in pain.

"Easy, boy," Lauren said, gripping his ankle to hold him in place just as much as to keep her balance.

"I don't like you taking care of me," he said.

"Then stop leaving me no other choice."

CHAPTER 13

ANOTHER TWO WEEKS PASSED MUCH THE SAME AS THE FIRST one had. Lauren grew more comfortable with both the dogs and their master, but still didn't fully understand either. This led her to focus much of her energy on something she could hopefully understand with the right information.

Her father's past.

Each day she'd finished her handler duties earlier and earlier. She'd found several ways of her own to exercise the dogs more effectively—from starting them at the bottom of the valley and having them pull her and the weighted sled uphill to putting Shane's car in neutral and having the bigger dogs pull it instead of the much smaller sled. Even Shane seemed impressed whenever she tromped back into the house before nightfall.

Today she'd woken up a couple hours earlier than usual

and was able to clock out around noon. This left the better part of the day at her disposal, and she knew just how she wanted to spend it.

Shane agreed to let her borrow his car so that she could drive into Anchorage and spend the afternoon touring the city. What he didn't know is that this was a research trip. She'd already ruminated over the facts she knew at length. Each day as she worked the dogs, she tried to connect the data points she knew by using the invisible lines she had yet to draw.

Today she would sharpen her mental pencil and maybe even solve the mystery altogether. She'd written down a timeline of events using the old newspaper articles and other mementos in the memory box. The first article was dated 1992, and the most recent one was 1995. She'd been two years old then but couldn't remember ever living in Alaska—nor had her father ever mentioned it. In fact, her birth certificate said she'd been born in California.

Was that even true?

Her mother had died when she was two. Was that the reason why her father had denied his former life and moved to New York to start over? But still, why would he keep it secret when he knew how much she craved every detail he could give about her late mother?

And why hide such a big part of himself?

That was as far as she could get on her own. She always

dead-ended on these major questions, feeling more confused than ever.

That's why today's mission was so important.

She started her tour of Anchorage at the practice grounds frequently mentioned in the articles about her father and the races. Sure enough, a number of sleds were out that day, dogs and men both racing cheerily around the track.

Lauren waited in the parking lot for someone to finish and pack up to go home. It didn't take long before a woman about her age appeared with a single dog at her side.

"Hi. Can I ask you a question?" Lauren said, striding up to her, trying to appear confident but not like a traveling saleswoman or some kind of petition pusher.

She shrugged and instructed her dog—an enormous black brindle Akita—to sit with a quick flip of the wrist. "I guess so. Not sure I'll have a good answer, but shoot."

"Thank you so much." Lauren hugged her notebook to her chest and reached out to shake the girl's hand. "I'm Lauren Dalton, and I'm here trying to learn about my father. He was a racer back in the 90's."

"I wasn't a racer in the 90's. Actually, I was born in the 90's."

"Me too," Lauren said with a laugh. "Are you a racer now?"

The girl shook her head. "Nope. Samson here likes the

trails, and we live so close by, we come here to do most of our walking."

"Oh." Lauren could feel the corners of her mouth tug down.

"But we're around racers enough to know the high points. What was your father's name?"

"Edward Dalton?" Lauren said it like a question, even though it was not.

She shook her head, seeming genuinely sad about not being able to help. "It sounds kind of familiar, but not familiar enough for me to give you what you're looking for."

"Well, thank you for your time. I'm sorry to have bothered you."

"No, that's okay. I just hope you find what you're looking for." She gestured for her dog to stand at her side and tightened the leash in her grip.

Lauren turned to see if there were any other people coming toward the parking lot. Maybe the next would have some answers for her.

But the girl with the Akita called her back. "Wait!"

Lauren turned, a fresh ray of hope shining in her heart.

"Have you tried asking at Loussac?" she said, idly petting her dog's head as she waited for Lauren's answer.

"No. Is that another trail grounds?"

The girl laughed. "No, it's the library. They keep all kinds of old articles and memorabilia. Actually, one of the librarians there is a friend of mine, and she's kind of obsessed with all things racing. Maybe she'll have some information on your father."

The library. Of course!

"Thank you for your help," Lauren shouted before rushing back toward her car and revving up the engine. She didn't realize until she was pulling back on the main road that she'd forgotten to ask the friendly stranger for her name.

CHAPTER 14

THE ZJ LOUSSAC PUBLIC LIBRARY LOOKED MORE LIKE A HIGH school than anything. With rounded architecture and crazy modern sculptures, this hardly felt like the place to uncover the secrets of the past. It felt more like a time machine into the future. Hadn't HG Wells written a book like that?

Lauren's father had always been a huge fan of science fiction novels, even though she hadn't read more than were required of her to get a passing grade in twelfth grade English. Had he once set foot inside this place, too?

Lauren swept into the building on a gust of cold wind, almost as if her father's ghost was urging her forward. Maybe he'd meant to share this past with her but had never found the right time.

How she wished he were still here—for this reason and

many more. When your entire world shatters at once, it's never really possible to pick up all the scattered pieces again. Was she no better than Shane with his broken vase, tirelessly kicking at the shards left behind and expecting them to form some kind of whole?

No.

She liked to think her intentions were nobler—and saner—than that. Her father would have wanted her to know. Surely he'd planned to tell her soon. Maybe even invite her up to Anchorage to explore his old stomping grounds. She wasn't supposed to be here alone.

The library interior was every bit as intimidating as its exterior. Maybe even more. She found herself amidst a strange hodgepodge of both old and new. When had libraries transformed into tech centers? Why couldn't books be enough to satisfy knowledge seekers?

She shook off her discomfort and headed to the large reception desk before her. Two workers manned the desk, though the older of the two pretended not to notice as Lauren approached.

The younger girl smiled brightly and placed the books she'd been scanning aside to greet their patron. "Hello!" she sang merrily. "How can we help you?"

Was this the librarian who the girl with the Akita had told her about?

The senior staffer continued to click things on the computer and pretend that Lauren didn't exist. Other than Shane, this was the coldest reception she'd received since setting foot in Alaska. It felt oddly out of place.

But the young librarian smiled even more broadly and repeated, "Can I help somehow?"

"Yes, do you have any old copies of the Times?"

"Sure, we do! Do you need Anchorage or New York?"

"Anchorage, please."

"And how old are we talking?"

"1992-1995."

"Oooh, that means we get to dig into the microfiche," the girl exclaimed. Her blonde hair was almost as pale as the snow outside, providing a stark contrast to her bright and rosy cheeks and her heavily glossed lips. Other than the lipstick, she wore no makeup, as far as Lauren could tell.

"Follow me," she said, stepping out from behind the desk and beckoning Lauren to follow her. "By the way, I'm Scarlett."

"I'm Lauren. Hi." She reached to offer her hand, which the librarian pumped enthusiastically in greeting.

"Hello!" Wow, Scarlett was an animated one. The effect was enhanced even more by her clothes, which were every bit as bright as her hair and skin were fair. She wore a purple blouse with navy green khakis and pink boots. Lauren had to admire her courage for putting together such an ensemble, especially since it worked.

Scarlett chattered the entire journey into the back of the library and led Lauren into a small, dark room. She flicked on the lights and marched down one of the aisles, trailing her finger on the labels of boxes as she went.

"Ah-ha!" she cried, finding the one she was looking for. She pulled it down and brought it over to a table with a super old computer-like thing sitting on top of it.

"Check this stuff out," she said, pulling out one of the microfiche sheets and squinting at it in the light. "Neat, right?"

"Sure," Lauren said with a laugh. "We'll go with neat."

Scarlett loaded up the first sheet and turned the screen on. "Are you here for a school project?"

Lauren shook her head. "No, I'm done with school. This is a family history project, I guess."

"Oooh, genealogy. That is one of my favorite things. Right after the great race, of course." Yes, this was definitely the librarian she'd heard tell of at the trails.

"Funny you should say that," Lauren confessed. "Because my father was a racer once, and I'm trying to learn about him. And I guess I'm kind of in the business, too. I recently signed up as a handler for Shane Ramsey. Have you heard of him?"

"Shane Ramsey?" Scarlett's cheeks grew redder still. "Oh, yes. Everyone has heard of him. I have some of his old gear, actually."

"Here? At the library? Can I see it?" Maybe she could make progress on the Shane mystery while she was here, too. Two birds with one stone at its finest.

Scarlett shifted her gaze back to the stacks. "No, not here. I have a collection at home. Racing memorabilia and other things like that."

"What kind of things?" Lauren asked, at once enchanted and overwhelmed by the vivacious librarian.

"Oh, all sorts of things! I have snow hooks and harnesses and gang lines and claw breaks and, well, you get the idea. Sometimes I try to play off how obsessed I am with racing when talking to normal people." Scarlett shrugged and rolled her eyes, making her a bit more approachable.

"Don't worry. Your secret's safe with me. Besides, I am far from being normal."

They both laughed. "That's good. I guess it means we can be friends."

"Sure, I could always use more friends, especially those who know so much about the kinds of things I'm trying to learn for myself."

Scarlett stayed with her while she continued to search through the microfiche, but neither found anything more than what Lauren already had from the box. When it was time to go, they exchanged numbers and promised to be in touch. Lauren even said she would have Scarlett up to meet Shane, suspecting that her new friend might have something of a little crush on him.

Lauren found it too funny to actually be jealous.

CHAPTER 15

LAUREN RETURNED HOME TOO LATE TO COOK DINNER, BUT having been prepared for this, she picked up a couple of combos from the Carl's Jr. drive thru to appease Shane. And, strangely, though she'd been expecting a confrontation, she found him in his best mood yet.

"Welcome back!" he said with a smile as she entered.

Lauren waited for a sarcastic comment or condescending question, but neither came. He seemed genuinely happy to see her tonight. "Did you miss me?" she asked, trying to draw out the true man she knew.

He set the book he'd been reading in his lap and looked up at her. "You know, it was actually way too quiet without you here. I hadn't realized how used to you I've gotten these past few weeks."

"So is that a yes, then?" she asked as she walked past him into the kitchen to grab a couple paper plates.

"It's an I guess so, which is kind of like a yes," he answered.

She plopped one of the burgers and a side of fries onto his plate and handed it over, then sat in the other recliner beside him.

"How'd you know I was craving Carl's Jr.?" he asked before taking a huge bite of his sandwich.

Lauren watched him in silence, waiting for the jab.

"Thank you," he enthused between bites.

"Okay," she said, rising back to her feet and putting her hands on her hips. "Who are you, and what have you done with old Mr. Grump?"

He laughed, but continued to eat. "I'm just happy today, I guess."

"Happy?"

He nodded.

"Happy?"

"Yes, happy."

"That's a word you know?" she demanded.

He rolled his deep blue eyes. "What? It's not like I'm never in a good mood."

"Yes, it is. That's exactly what it's like."

"Point taken." He laughed and started to munch away at his fries. "I'll try harder to play nice."

Lauren wanted to continue to argue, but she also knew better than to question this divine gift of providence. Maybe she and Shane Ramsey could be friends after all. How about that?

They chatted about their days as they finished off their meals. All of it was so surprisingly pleasant that Lauren almost had to pinch herself to make sure it was real. Okay, as nice as this was, she had to know why.

"Shane?" she asked.

"Hmm?" He looked up at her, truly looked at her, not just through her or past her like usual. She liked how it felt. More and more, she could understand Scarlett's little crush. Shane was a handsome man when he wasn't spoiling it with his awful personality.

This version of Shane was definitely one she could get behind, but was it the real him?

"I have to know..." she ventured, kicking up the footrest and leaning back in her chair. "What happened today? Why are you in such a good mood?"

"It's just a good day," he said.

"A good day, okay. Did you win the lottery? Is it your birthday? Something else I should know about?"

He laughed and set back his chair as well. "Nothing like that. Just a good day and a good book."

She looked to his lap and tried to read the cover, but the light reflecting from the overhead fixture obscured it from her prying eye. "Ahh, so that book is making you happy. What kind of book is it?"

"I already told you, it's a good book. One of my favorites, actually."

"Well, there you go, being difficult again. I knew this couldn't last. Are you going to tell me about this good, mood-altering book or not?"

Shane pushed his chair back into its upright position and handed the book over to her. "Are you so sure it's me who's the difficult one? It's not the book that's making me happy but, here, take a look. You can even read it when I'm done if you want."

She accepted the tattered paperback which she suspected had been read more than one time and on more than one good day. The cover was mostly dark and had a black-and-white picture of the author at its center. The Collected Works of Jack London. "Is this the guy who wrote Call of the Wild?" she asked. "I think I read that in high school."

"Yup. It's a—"

"Good book," she finished for him. "I know. You've mentioned that, nerd."

"You're the one who spent all day in the library," he pointed out. "Okay, so if you're too good for Jack London, then what do you like to read?"

"Oh, almost anything I can get my hands on, but mostly romance."

Shane made a fake gagging noise and Lauren threw his precious book back at him. It hit his chest with a thud.

"Stop that!" she cried. "Romance is awesome and you have no right to make fun of it."

"That stuff is for girls, not big, strapping men like me." He puffed out his chest like a smarmy rooster.

"First of all, I am a girl, and second of all, that is one-hundred-percent not true. Saying romance is for girls is like saying love is just for girls. That one of the most important human experiences isn't meant to be experienced by half of humanity. Haven't you ever been in love?"

The energy in the room shifted so fast it made Lauren nauseous.

"Love," Shane said with a huff. "No one could ever love me."

With an attitude like that, you're not wrong, Lauren thought but didn't say aloud.

CHAPTER 16

LAUREN HAD INTENDED TO GO BACK TO HER ORIGINAL schedule with the dogs, but waking up early one day apparently meant she'd need to wake up early every day going forward—or find a way to sleep through two solid hours of happy barking. She'd never needed a lot of sleep to get by, so she chose the former.

Besides, it was nice being done with her work for the day by noon. This gave her time to work both toward solving her mysteries and to figuring out what she'd do next when Shane recovered fully and no longer needed her services as a handler.

Sometimes she thought that she might like to settle here in Alaska—not the tiny hamlet of Puffin Ridge, but rather the more vibrant, alive city of Anchorage. Maybe she would get her own team of dogs and become a racer herself. That idea did appeal to her more and more as she became acclimated to this way of life. Still, she had no idea what would come next.

In fact, the only thing she knew for sure was that there was no going back, not to data corp, and not to the way her life had been before.

She needed to continue to find a way forward. She was determined to.

Now that she knew how to get to town and had extra time in her day, she'd also started learning more about cooking. While she didn't love the process, she loved the result. And whether or not he would say it, Shane did, too.

Today she'd planned a hearty three-bean soup cooked in the small slow cooker she'd picked up on her last visit to town. When she came in from working the dogs, the cabin already smelled of caramelized onions and stewed carrots, an aroma that made her stomach leap in joyful anticipation.

Shane was awake and sitting at the table by the window as he normally did this time of day. While he would usually have his tablet with him as he read over the news, today he had company.

A handsome man with sandy brown hair and a clean-shaven face sat chatting with him over shared mugs of coffee. Something about him looked familiar, but Lauren couldn't quite place him.

The man seemed to know her instantly, though, rising

to his feet and offering his hand in greeting the moment she stepped into the kitchen.

"Lauren, hello! Seems like things are working out great here. I'm so happy you found the SDRO and that we were able to get Shane and his dogs the help they needed. How are you enjoying the new job?" He smiled broadly, waiting for recognition to light in her eyes.

SDRO? Ahh, the Sled Dog Rescue Organization. So this must be one of the higher ups. The man she'd spoken to on the phone when she'd first called in about the position was a veterinarian, Lolly Winston's husband. Was this him?

He caught the confusion in her gaze. "I guess we've never met in person, huh? I'm Oscar Rockwell, co-director of the SDRO. I handle the dogs' care and technical sides of the charity, while my wife Lolly runs our PR."

"Of course," Lauren said warmly. This man was a saint to give so much of his life to helping others, especially to helping animals. "It's nice to meet you in person."

Oscar offered her his chair and went to find a spare for himself, leaving her and Shane alone for a few brief moments.

"Did you know he was coming today?" she asked.

Shane shook his head. "No, it's a surprise check-in. They do it when they place a dog, but I hadn't realized they'd be checking in on us as well. It seems my reputation precedes me."

She raised an eyebrow at him, working hard to hold back the laugh that tickled at her throat. "As a grump, you mean?"

He nodded and took a sip from his mug. It had a field of large, hand-painted flowers splashed across the side and seemed unlike his usual choices in decor. She wondered if it had been a gift he'd clung to all these years—and if so, who might have given it to him.

Oscar returned with a chair, bringing his bright energy back to the otherwise dim cabin. "I couldn't help but overhear," he said. "I promise I'm only here to see how you're doing and if there's any way I or the organization can help. *Not* to play judge and jury."

"Well, that's a relief," Shane said with a quick shake of the head. "I was afraid you'd come to take my new handler away."

"Nobody can take me anywhere I don't want to go," Lauren pointed out. "Unlike the dogs, I can make my own decisions."

"Totally true," Oscar affirmed. "And you remind me of my no-nonsense wife, which tells me you can handle this guy fine enough on your own."

Lauren blushed at the compliment. She wondered if one day she might get to meet Lolly and maybe grab an autograph while she was at it.

Shane smirked and wiped his mouth with the back of his hand before setting his cup back onto the table. "No nonsense is absolutely right. This one sure does give me a run for my money."

"Oh?" Oscar asked, setting his mug back down onto a clear patch of table. Shane's papers still littered most of the surface, and it killed Lauren that she couldn't just clean them up on his behalf.

"Oh yes, she doesn't take crap from anyone, least of all me. The dogs love her and recognize her as an authority figure now, though that took some doing. I wasn't sure at first, you know, that such a rookie could actually be anything more than a pain in my backside, but she's proven herself little by little." He glanced briefly toward Lauren before turning his full attention back to the visiting vet.

He did like her. He did think she was doing a good job. She hadn't known for sure until now and, boy, did it feel good to receive that validation from her grumpy, difficult-to-please employer.

"So that's why the complaint emails stopped coming in?" Oscar asked, running a finger around the rim of his now empty mug.

Lauren wanted to hear what Shane had to say for himself, but she also needed to make sure their guest was well taken care of. She popped to her feet and grabbed the coffee pot from the far counter while continuing to listen to the men's exchange.

Shane dropped his voice a couple notches, but she could

still hear him clear as day. "What do you expect when you send me someone with zero experience? But, yes, it worked out in the end. All's good here. In fact, I've been thinking about signing her and the dogs up for a race sometime soon. You know, to keep the dogs in shape mostly."

Mostly? What were his other reasons? Lauren wondered.

"Well, I'm glad to hear all that," Oscar said as Lauren topped off his coffee. "You know I'm just a phone call away if you ever need me. That goes for both of you. While I'm here, do you mind if I check in on the dogs too?"

"Be my guest," Shane said. "They'll be happy to see you."

They both watched Oscar suit up in his winter gear and head outside to the kennels, taking his freshly replenished coffee with him. When the door shut behind him, Lauren said, "Thank you for saying all those nice things. It would have been nice to hear them earlier, but I guess beggars can't be choosers."

"Don't let it get to your head," he mumbled, raising his cup again and watching through the window as Oscar made his way over to the dogs. "You still have a long way to go, but at least you're finally moving."

"Whatever, Mr. Grump. You like me, no use denying it now."

"What a loaded word," he said with a smile.

"It's okay. I like you, too." She grabbed a cup of coffee for herself, and they sat together in companionable silence for a while longer before both returned to their separate daily routines.

It was days like this that Lauren truly felt as if she'd found a home.

CHAPTER 17

SHANE CAME TO DINNER THAT EVENING WITH AN AGENDA. AT least, that's the way Lauren saw it.

She served up piping hot bowls of her homemade soup, which they decided to take to the pair of recliners in the living room and eat by the fire. Shane always seemed to open up most when they were sitting there together, almost as if removing the physical obstacle of the table also tore down some kind of emotional barrier, too.

In front of the fire, he bared his soul. From discussing books to chatting about their respective days, all the way to the good-natured ribbing that so often took place between the two of them, the flames seemed to give him courage while the comfort of the recliner relieved his many hidden anxieties.

"This is good soup," he said to her after trying the first

spoonful. "I've noticed you're spending a lot more time in the kitchen. Do you think you might apply to be a cook once you're done here?" Shane took another noisy slurp of the broth to emphasize his appreciation.

She shrugged. "Honestly, I don't know what I'll do next. Trying to take it one day at a time."

He frowned and set his bowl on the side table, turning toward her with something that resembled pity in his eyes. "Taking it one day at a time is a recipe for disaster. It means you're running a race without knowing whether there's a finish line."

"It's life. Of course there's a finish line. And, really, what more can I do?" she asked, shifting away from his intense gaze. "We don't know how long it will be until you get better and don't need me anymore. Who knows what I'll want by then." She hoped he'd take this opportunity to reveal what he wanted. Perhaps he could create a more permanent position for her. Maybe she wouldn't have to leave, and maybe he didn't want her to go.

He didn't say any of that. Instead, he simply stated, "I suggest you figure out what you want."

"What? So I can be happy like you? Don't make me laugh." His lack of passion rankled her. She knew he had begun to like her. He'd made it obvious that morning. So why was he so stubbornly insistent on acting this way?

Lauren stirred her soup, staring into the browns, oranges, and greens as they whirled around the bowl together.

"Then don't be so stupid," Shane continued, obviously unamused, unmoved, un*anything*. "If you don't take charge now, you could end up living a life you never wanted, one you don't like very much."

"Is that from experience?"

"Maybe."

"Care to elaborate?"

"No." He leaned back in his chair and closed his eyes as if to shut her out.

"Then maybe don't offer advice you can't back up," she grumbled. The deliciousness of their meal had already been ruined by this insane battle. She'd really thought they'd reached a turning point in their relationship, but apparently she'd been wrong. Had it all been a show for Oscar Rockwell, or was Shane really this hot and cold all the time?

"I'm not trying to upset you." His eyes were still closed as he spoke.

Lauren huffed. For someone who wasn't trying to upset her, he did a fantastic job of it. Shane Ramsey knew just how to get under her skin. He'd known it from the beginning.

"Listen," he urged, "I'm trying to help here. Just... Don't rely on me, okay? If you need to put in notice, do it. If you need to go somewhere else, go. Don't let me and the dogs hold you back. It may seem like it's just a matter of a few months, but what if these few months end up ruining the rest of your life?"

She rolled her eyes, ready for this conversation to be over. Every time she felt them becoming closer, he pulled away again. "It's a temp job, Shane. We both know that. It's what I need right now, so unless this is your way of firing me, can we please change the topic?"

"Have it your way." He opened his eyes again, the blues revitalized by the brief rest. She could get lost in those eyes. Maybe she already had.

CHAPTER 18

A FEW MORE DAYS PASSED, DURING WHICH SHANE GREW increasingly distant. Sure, he was *there*. He was *always there*, but he'd closed back up the part of himself that he'd only briefly shown to Lauren, leaving her to wonder if he might be trying to force her hand, to make her quit for some unknown reason.

Lauren didn't like playing games, especially ones of which she couldn't even begin to understand the rules. But *he* was every bit as stubborn as *she* was determined, which left them at an impasse.

One afternoon, she'd initially planned to drive into Puffin Ridge and run a few errands. All that changed, however, when the flame-haired Grace arrived to shuttle Shane to his appointment in the city.

"I have a doctor's appointment, plus some business to

tend to in the city today," he explained as they both watched Grace breeze from her car to the front door of the cabin. She wondered why he couldn't just take himself since he was fully capable of driving on his own. Did the doctor give him drugs that rendered him unable to operate heavy machinery? If so, what and why?

"If you really needed a chauffeur, I could have taken you. I'm free," she argued, but he just shrugged.

"It's quite all right," the physical therapist explained, having heard the last part of their conversation after letting herself in. "I don't mind helping out."

Shane nodded. "Grace always takes me to these things. No need to change something that works."

"We'll be gone for several hours at least. So don't wait up," Grace said with a laugh as she escorted Shane and his crutches through the doorway.

Well, if that was the way he wanted it, Lauren could find plenty to keep her busy with the entire cabin at her disposal. There was still much she needed to know, and if Shane wasn't going to tell her, then she'd have to figure things out another way.

It's not snooping, she reasoned, *if I'm doing it for a good cause. If I understand what has him so down all the time, then maybe I can help.*

And she knew just where to start—the old garden shed out back. Then again, perhaps if Shane caught her in the act, he'd be angry enough to at least show some emotion toward her again.

As much as she missed their heated arguments, she didn't want their hard-earned relationship to regress. The fact that they now stood still drove her crazy. The right bit of intel, though, could change everything—make it better for both of them.

She waited a half an hour, just to make sure the coast was truly clear. She decided that a credit card, kitchen knife, and bobby pin would be the most useful tools for working the lock and brought them with her outside. She tried the bobby pin last, because it required taking off her gloves in the chill air. But the heavy knob refused to budge. Nothing worked, and likely nothing would work except the designated key.

Perhaps if she searched, she could find it mixed in with Shane's things inside?

Feeling a new sense of determination, she tromped back in and started with the kitchen. Well, as long as she was going through things, she may as well organize them, too.

The papers on the kitchen table had remained scattered for the weeks since she'd arrived, and it was driving her crazy. Surely he wouldn't mind if she sorted them into neat stacks? That wasn't too intrusive, was it?

She scanned each paper quickly to determine which pile was best to place it in. Mostly, she found the standard kinds of mail: bills, licenses, advertisements, and even an old court summons.

The summons gave nothing away, but it did make Lauren wonder, had Shane been in some kind of lawsuit? Or had he committed a misdemeanor? Lost his temper and assaulted someone? Whatever the case, it was more than three years old, and the matter had likely been long since resolved.

Feeling satisfied with her work at the table, she moved on to the junk drawer, which seemed the most likely place someone would hide a spare key. But unlike every other surface in the house, the junk drawer was neatly organized with things like tape, scissors, tools, a tape measurer—all in their clearly marked places.

Strange.

She took a deep breath and headed toward the only other place in the house she wasn't supposed to go: Shane's bedroom. What could possibly be in there that needed to be kept a secret? He didn't seem the type to blush over his boxers, which meant something really good had to be concealed back there.

Maybe he had a memory box or two of his own.

She looked out the window one more time to make sure she was totally alone, then turned the knob, took a deep breath, and let herself into Shane's bedroom.

CHAPTER 19

SHE'D EXPECTED TO FIND A MESS OF DISCARDED CLOTHES, OLD takeout containers, and other debris, but Shane's bedroom, unlike the rest of the house, sat neat and tidy. The walls were painted a dark red and all the blinds were drawn tightly shut, making the place feel more like a cave than anything. Was this where Shane went to hibernate and shut out the rest of the world, including her?

She understood that, but she couldn't figure out why he'd made such a point to keep her out until now. The room held nothing remarkable—a king-sized bed, long dresser, and even a tiny ceiling-mounted TV with a VHS player built right in. She had to wonder if that old thing still worked and if Shane actually had the right kind of tapes to play in it.

Everything was dark—the wood, the walls, the bedding, even the ceiling was painted black as night. It all seemed at odds with the rest of the house. Was this how the secret shed was decorated, too?

She drifted over to the dresser. A coin dish, bottle of cologne, and can of spray deodorant were the only items that sat on its surface. The absence of dust implied that Shane regularly cleaned—but why in here and not the rest of the house?

The weight of her guilt loomed thick like fog, and Lauren said a quick prayer to ask for forgiveness for encroaching on Shane's privacy like this. Still, she pushed forward in her search. The betrayal had already happened, and she couldn't have it be for nothing. She needed to see what she could find.

Inside the dresser, she found neatly folded clothing and carefully matched socks, none of which she'd ever seen her employer wear. They were going out clothes, yet he never went much of anywhere these days and preferred pajamas for around home. Even for his appointment today, he wore sweats and an old T-shirt. Nothing fancy.

In the closet, she found a handsome navy suit, the kind she'd often seen execs wearing back in New York. Finely polished Oxfords lined the floor of the closet, and a series of dress shirts hung from the rod. She even found a collection of ascots kept neatly in a lidless wooden box.

It was almost as if Shane had a second life as a high-powered stockbroker or an old-fashioned crooner... even as a news anchor or gangster. She couldn't see Shane in any of those roles, though. She couldn't picture him any other way than he was now, which made this discovery all the more unsettling.

Above the clothes, a high shelf drew her curiosity. It was more than six feet from the floor, and while she could clearly see that something was wedged in the back, she couldn't reach it without finding something to stand on first.

Okay, once she figured out what was up there, she'd stop snooping once and for all. Her investigation today had yielded more questions than answers, which helped neither her nor Shane. She wasn't any closer to understanding his thinly masked pain. In fact, she felt like she'd wandered into the secret lair of Dr. Jekyll and Mr. Hyde. Was it possible that there wasn't just one real Shane but two? And which version had *she* become acquainted with?

She grabbed a chair from the kitchen and returned to the closet, feeling more than ready to put this all behind her.

Unfortunately, that was when the front door swung open with a low, ominous creak.

Oh no!

What was he doing home so early?

Grace had said they'd be out for hours. And where could Lauren hide so that Shane wouldn't spot her, and she could slip away later... perhaps if he went to use the bathroom or visit with the dogs outside.

Think, think, think.

But there wasn't time for that. Lauren tucked herself in the closet. Unfortunately, she didn't have the time or space to take the repurposed kitchen chair with her.

Crap, crap, crap!

Shane came in then. She could see him through the thin opening between the closet doors, and he did not look happy. His eyes landed right on the chair and his face darkened to match the rest of the room. "Lauren!" he bellowed.

"Yes?" she squeaked, slowly opening the closet and stepping into the main part of the master suite.

"What are you doing in my room? You know you're not supposed to be in here," he demanded, fixing her with a heated stare.

"I know, I'm sorry. I just—"

"You just nothing! Get out! Get out now!" He screamed so loud, the air shook and emitted a high pitch sound that echoed through the house's wiring.

"Shane, let me explain. I—"

"No, you don't get to explain. You only need to get out." He pointed toward the open door emphatically and stared wide-eyed at her as if his eyes could physically move her from the space.

"I didn't see anything, I swear. I didn't know—"

"You knew you weren't supposed to come in here, but that's just like you, isn't it?" His expression turned sinister.

"You're always doing whatever you want, regardless of the rules. Well, you know what? I'm done. *You're* done."

"Wait, no. Are you firing me?"

Shane let out an angry string of curses. "Why are you still in my room? *Get out!*" The same tremor she'd spotted when he'd made the mess of the flowers had returned. His entire chest heaved as if he were desperately short of breath.

She wanted to apologize, wanted to explain, but what could she say? She had invaded his privacy, and she'd done it knowingly.

"I'm so sorry. What I did was wrong, and I—" Taking a chance, she walked toward him and placed her hand on his arm, but he ripped it away as if he'd been burned.

"Don't touch me. Don't touch my things. Don't even talk to me. Just get out! I expect you to be gone when I wake up in the morning. You're no longer welcome here."

Lauren wanted to get angry. She wanted to meet Shane's screams with her own, but this time, she knew she was in the wrong, had known all along.

Would the dogs suffer because her curiosity got the best of her? And what of Shane? Though he was raging like a beast again, he'd become her friend. Would he be able to focus on getting better without the added help? And where would she go?

She had no idea, but she knew this was what she deserved.

"Get out right now before I get you out myself." Shane seethed and, despite his red-hot rage, she knew he could never hurt her. Words were his weapon of choice, and even then, he avoided saying anything he couldn't take back later.

But he'd fired her. Would he take that back? Or was this it? And which way did she prefer?

"Not going to listen, are you?" He reached for her waist to pick her up, but Lauren shifted out of his grasp and moved into the hall.

When the door slammed in her face, she felt a hot rush of tears stream down her cheeks.

What was she going to do now?

CHAPTER 20

LAUREN SAT IN SHOCK FOR WHAT FELT LIKE HOURS. SHE'D gone and ruined everything for everyone. There wasn't any way around that.

But why did it matter so much to her? Why couldn't she just leave Shane to his secrets and move on? And why did the thought of leaving rip her heart in two?

It's the dogs, she told herself. *I love those dogs. They need me, and I need them.*

Maybe she could find a new position as handler for a different, more even-tempered racer. She doubted Shane would give her a good recommendation after tonight's showdown—and she could hardly blame him.

Ridiculous or not, the man had his boundaries, and she'd tried far too many times to cross them. This was what she deserved, and if she was being honest with herself, it would have happened sooner or later anyway.

This was why Lauren had always found it difficult to figure out what she wanted from life. The things she felt most passionate about in one moment often ended up as flavor of the month rather than a lasting taste. It wasn't healthy, and it wasn't good for anybody—least of all herself.

Up here in the wilds of Alaska, she'd learned a hard lesson at the hands of Shane Ramsey, and now it was time to move on to the next thing... *Whatever that was.*

She wiped the last of the tears from her cheeks and dragged her suitcase onto the bed so that she could pack up what was left of her life.

A soft knock sounded on the door—so soft, she couldn't be sure she heard anything at all.

The knock came again, louder, surer. "Can I come in?" Shane's voice floated through the door, and Lauren felt the tears well up all over again.

"Okay," she said with a shaky voice she hardly recognized as her own.

Shane stood awkwardly in the doorway, refusing to cross the threshold, a courtesy she had failed to give him.

"Well?" she asked when he said nothing.

He talked to a spot on the floor rather than to her, but his voice was soft and kind. "I'm sorry I lost my cool in there."

"It is what it is." She shrugged, trying to play it cool in case he looked up and saw her patchy cheeks and red eyes. She couldn't bring herself to apologize again because, truth be told, they'd both done wrong. He was every bit as guilty as she was in this scenario.

"Maybe," he offered, taking a small step into the room, almost as if he were afraid to enter. They'd both said sorry, so why was he still here? She hated that he was dragging this out. She just wanted to be done; it was the only way she'd ever begin to feel better about it.

His voice faltered. "I... I didn't mean what I said."

"But you said it."

"You don't have to go."

"You fired me, remember?"

"I do." He paused as if rehearsing his words first in his head. "Lauren..." he started, and she wondered if she'd actually ever heard him use her name before. She liked the way it sounded coming from his mouth and realized, in that moment, he had come to mean so much more to her than just an employer, just a grump.

"Lauren," he repeated, "I shouldn't have made those house rules. I shouldn't have made you feel like a stranger in a place that is supposed to be your home. I shouldn't have lost my temper, and I shouldn't have fired you."

"But you did. You did all those things. Why?" Her voice started shaking again, and she wondered if he would take her into his arms to comfort her. But, no, of course not. Whatever these feelings were, they were hers and hers alone. She wasn't sure that Shane Ramsey had ever loved anyone or anything for a single day in his miserable life.

He took another step closer and hung his head, looking up at her from beneath dark lashes. "I can't tell you that."

Her frustration swelled. They'd come back to this again. Even if she decided to stay, could he ever fully let her in? "Why? Why not? Why do you keep so many secrets and then expect me not to go looking for answers?"

"That's fair," he said. "But please understand, I just... I can't, Lauren." He said her name again, a supplication, a prayer for understanding.

But would she answer it?

"I don't know, Shane." She shook her head and returned to packing her suitcase. "Every time I think we're making progress, something like this happens. I'm sick of feeling like an outsider, like someone you put up with because you have no choice. I know if you had it your way, you'd be fully recovered tomorrow and I'd be shipped back to New York in a heartbeat."

He groaned and leaned back against the wall as if he suddenly couldn't support his own weight—not even with the help of the crutches. "What did you think this was? It's a job, one you do well, but it's still... it's just a job."

"Is that all I am to you? An employee?"

"It's all you can ever be. Please understand. *It's not you. It's me.*"

"Okay, now I'm really confused. Are you breaking up with me or firing me?"

He laughed, and it sounded unnatural in that moment. "How about neither? Please stay. The dogs need you. I need you."

She crossed her arms and sank onto the bed, already knowing in her heart that she would stay as long as he needed her, as long as he still wanted her. "You have a funny way of showing it."

"I know… So you'll stay?"

"Yes, but this can't happen again, Shane. Any sane woman would have hightailed it the moment you lost your temper like that."

He stood upright again and came closer, but did not join her on the bed. His words were gentle as he asked, "Then why didn't you?"

She reached up and grabbed his hand, squeezing it inside her own. "Because you're my friend."

He didn't pull away, but he didn't return the pressure either. "How did that happen?"

"I honestly have no idea, but as your friend, I'm going to call you out when you're being an irrational jerk."

He gave her hand a quick squeeze before letting go. "I'd expect nothing less. Will you please stop packing now?"

She zipped her suitcase shut and placed it back in the corner of the room. "Now get out of my room before I lose my temper," she joked, feeling like a million pounds had been lifted from her shoulders.

CHAPTER 21

WHEN LAUREN WOKE UP THE NEXT MORNING, SHANE WAS already out and about—and full of energy, too.

"Good morning, sleepyhead!" he said as he hefted a giant pack onto the kitchen table. His crutches wobbled beneath his arms, but he stood strong.

"Sleepyhead?" Before she could stop it, her mouth stretched wide in an audible yawn. "Is that my new nickname?"

"It's only fair with you calling me Mr. Grump all the time." He rummaged through his supplies and turned to Lauren with a satisfied smirk. "Well, hurry up and grab some breakfast. We've got a busy day ahead."

Lauren wasn't sure what she had expected in the wake of their huge blowup and mutual apology last night, but this probably wasn't it. She padded over to the refrigerator in her house slippers and grabbed a container of yogurt.

"You'll need to wear something comfortable," Shane added, searching back through his bag again. "And warm."

"I always dress warm and comfortable." She dipped her spoon into the yogurt and leaned back against the sink. "You gonna tell me what you have planned?"

"You'll find out soon enough. Now get dressed and help me load up the truck." He headed outside without her, which meant she needed to hurry through her morning routine if she were going to accompany him on whatever journey he had planned. And, oh, how she looked forward to this surprise!

Lauren had only ever seen Shane's car, so she was startled to hear him talk about a truck. She was even more surprised to find it outfitted with traveling cages for the dogs built right in. They stood two rows high on each side, with six cubbies per row facing outward, each housing open flaps for the dogs to stick their heads through. She helped Shane get the sled tied to the top of the truck, then watched in awe as he effortlessly lifted the dogs into their cubbies, a feat that was all the more impressive given his injury.

"We only need ten dogs today. We'll take the others on the next trip."

"Can we bring Briar Rose?" Lauren asked as Shane

helped Fred into one of the open kennels. "She's my favorite."

He laughed. "Fine, if you insist. She won't do us much good, but we have Alice as a spare, I suppose."

"Why not?" she asked, but Shane reached across her to open the passenger door without answering.

"Get in. You're driving."

In all her life, Lauren had never driven such a giant, hulking vehicle, but she was too excited about the mystery adventure to argue.

"Hope you can drive a stick," he said as they both buckled up.

"And if I can't?"

He laughed and shook his head. "Then you'll just have to figure it out. Not many folks on the road at this time anyway."

"Well, it's lucky I already know how then. I don't want to be responsible for killing ten of your finest dogs."

"Or me," he added.

She shrugged and rolled her eyes. This felt good, like the way they were always meant to communicate with each other.

"Okay, killer. Take it easy," Shane said, pointing out the window. "Take a right out of here and head toward Bay Road."

"You going to tell me where we're going?"

"I already told you, you'll find out soon enough. It's about an hour off."

"So no talking until then?" She did her best to focus on the road ahead, but the image of Shane in her periphery distracted her more than once.

"We can talk." He seemed relaxed this morning. Was he relaxed enough to open up? She had to try.

Only half joking, she turned to wink at him and said, "Okay, then tell me your mysterious secret, please."

"*Har har.* I don't think so, but now that you mention it, you haven't exactly shared your life story either."

She bit her upper lip, something she used to do all the time as a child before a retainer corrected her underbite. "That's because there's not much to tell."

"That doesn't really surprise me," he quipped.

"Hey! Wasn't part of being friends now making sure we're nice to each other?"

"Who's not being nice? I haven't said a mean thing to you all day."

She rolled her eyes again as they turned onto the highway. "Great job, considering it's already seven AM."

"You going to tell me your life story or what?"

"My entire life story? You really want to know the whole, long thing?"

"Okay, maybe not the whole thing, but you could start by telling me why you're here."

"Well..." She took a deep breath and let it out slowly to build the suspense. His eyes were glued to her now. Was he every bit as eager to learn about her as she was to learn about him? She might as well have a little fun with it by teasing him the way he so often teased her. "I'm here now because you told me I have to come with you to this mysterious destination. By the way, where are we going?"

"I don't think so, *Lauren*." A little shiver ran up her spine at the sound of her name on his lips yet again. "Really, why did you take this job with me?"

She confessed, "I'm trying to learn about my father, and this seemed like a good place to get started."

"Is your father Edward Dalton? I thought it was just a coincidence, your name. Didn't realize you actually have ice in your blood."

"You knew my father?" This entire time she could have asked Shane. Did he hold the keys not only to his own secrets, but to hers as well?

"I knew *of* your father," Shane clarified, and just as quickly as her hopes had risen toward the sky, they came plummeting back to earth—a sad, pathetic fallen star. "He was a great racer."

She sighed and gripped the steering wheel tighter.

"That's what I hear, but I didn't find out until he died earlier this year."

"Earlier this year? It's only February."

"I know." She took her eyes off the road a minute to look over at him.

"That explains a lot, actually."

"Like?" Had he figured her out because he was interested in learning about her as well, or was it just that she was so plainly transparent?

He fiddled with the shoulder strap on his seat belt as he spoke, almost as if the topic of Lauren's past made him nervous. "Why you showed up out of the blue with no experience. Why you insisted on staying when I tried to get rid of you. Why you seem sad sometimes."

She felt the hot sting of tears but refused to let them fall. She'd shed so many for her father already, but she also knew he wouldn't want her to be unhappy when remembering him. She forced a smile and said, "I miss him. Have you ever lost anyone you loved?"

Shane frowned. "I don't love, remember? And, besides, we're here."

Lauren studied him for a moment, and when it was clear that he would reveal no more, she turned to study the scene before them. Several trucks like their own stood in the open field. Men hefted sleds and other supplies from their trucks, and dogs whined as they were tied to their gang lines. The entire scene buzzed with excitement, and Lauren buzzed, too, looking out at it, knowing that soon she'd be among them.

He'd brought her to a race, her first ever, and a fresh chance to prove herself.

CHAPTER 22

"YOU REALLY MEANT IT," LAUREN WHISPERED AS THEY exited the truck and made their way back toward the cargo hold to get the dogs. "You weren't just saying it to make Dr. Rockwell happy. You've brought me to an actual race."

"When do I ever do anything with the express intention of making someone happy? Besides, this isn't a race. It's how mushers normally train. Welcome to the big leagues." She felt his eyes roving over her as he tried to gauge her reaction. "You got this?"

"I sure do," she answered on an exhale. "Thank you so much for this!" And before she could stop herself, she leapt into his arms and gave him a giant, enthusiastic hug.

He looked down at her. His face wore a mix of shock and pleasure. That was the moment Lauren knew for sure. Shane cared for her, too. His tough guy exterior wasn't the real him. The real Shane was the man she'd seen occasional glimpses of between all the heavily guarded moments that made up their life together.

He brushed her off and forced a laugh. "That's enough of that."

She almost said *sorry* before realizing she had nothing to apologize for. Instead, she gave him a second, quick followup squeeze and said, "Thank you so much. I won't let you down."

His cheeks turned red behind his new beard, and she wondered if it was from the cold or for something else. Were her cheeks red, too?

"Well," he said, kicking at a block of ice on the road. "Let's get the dogs hooked in. Go too slow and you'll be stuck out here all day. All night, too."

Shane tied the sled to a bent metal pipe sticking out of the ground and pulled out the snow hook, setting that in the ground, too.

"Worried the sled will slide away?" Lauren laughed.

He just smiled, a bit of a gleam in his eyes.

They worked together to place the ten dogs into a formation before the sled. Fred and Wendy were the biggest, so they were stationed closest to the sled.

"Our wheel dogs pull the hardest," Shane explained as each dog was tied into place. "These are the team dogs, the swing dogs, and finally the lead dogs. Your leads..." He pointed toward Lewis and Jack at the front of the line. "Will take care of you if you tell them the way to go. *Gee* is right, and *haw* is left. Got it?"

"Yup."

"Ready?"

She took a deep breath, and when she blew it out, tiny crystals formed in the air. "As I'll ever be." She glanced from the track back toward Shane, and he gave her a thumbs up.

Together, they guided the team toward the starting point. A few other racers lingered with their sleds, but it didn't seem like enough to offer a proper race.

She looked toward Shane.

"This is a training run to get our blood pumping, but mostly for us to check in with the competition. Make sure you hang a left at every fork in the trail so that we can give these dogs a good run. That should make about twenty-two miles. On this track, I average about two-forty-five to three with ten dogs. That's the time I want you to shoot for, too. These dogs can handle it. The question is, can you?" He pulled up the snow hook and placed it on the back of the basket.

Why did he keep asking her if she could do this? Hadn't she made that obvious already? She nodded up at him, and he clapped her on the back.

"Great. Now, step onto the foot boards and hang on tight."

The dogs whined and shifted in their harnesses, waiting for the command from Shane.

"By the way," he said. "I'll be at the tavern to catch up with some old friends. When you're done, get some of the men here to help you load up the truck, then head home. I'll see you there later tonight. Okay?"

He gave her another clap on the back, then untethered her sled from the starting pole. "Hike!" he shouted from behind her.

Just like that, the dogs, led by Jack and Lewis, pulled forward and the sled took off down the trail, picking up speed quickly as they approached the first bend in the trail. The wind whipped past her cheeks, blowing the little tendrils of hair that had escaped from beneath her knit cap. This was as close to flying as a person could get, she knew it —and loved it.

While working with the dogs back at the cabin, she'd only ever taken one out at a time, so she wasn't quite prepared for the intense speed, for how fast the world moved around her.

Prepared or not, the best way to learn was by doing. She gripped the handlebar tight and shifted her weight to the left or right as needed, occasionally stepping on the foot brake to slow the dogs at a turn and keep the line tight. She'd spent so much time practicing for this that her body seemed to know what to do before her brain had the time to figure it out.

Faster, faster, freer, freer.

Now she saw the outline of another musher farther up the trail. She was gaining on him. Could she actually match Shane's time—or better yet, beat it?

She was going to try.

She shouted "Hike, hike, hike" over the wind to encourage the dogs to pull harder, then hunched down low to minimize any wind resistance caused by her erect posture. She was smaller than the other racers, which meant the dogs could devote less energy toward pulling and more toward reaching top speeds.

"Mush, mush!" she cried to encourage the dogs further. She didn't know if that was the right command, but her words encouraged the dogs nonetheless.

They reached another turn in the trail and she leaned into the turn like she'd seen motorcycle riders do to help the sled take a sharp turn and maintain as much of their speed as possible on the curve.

Whack!

Lauren landed on a fresh bed of snow, her cheek and side stinging from the impact, but more than that, her ego. She watched as the dogs continued to pull the sled down the trail—not needing her to continue on their path.

Her entire side ached from the impact, but it didn't matter. She had to catch that sled!

She ran as hard as she could, but it was difficult in all the thick layers she'd bundled herself in, especially considering how much of her energy she'd already used on the sled.

The dogs rounded the track. The last trace of the sled, disappearing around the bend.

Shane was going to kill her.

CHAPTER 23

Lauren turned around and walked back to the starting grounds. Surely there was someone there who could help her. She thought about calling Shane, but he had only just begun to believe in her and she didn't want to ruin that already.

As she tromped the long way back to the trail head, the sky began to darken. Days were ridiculously short here. No sooner had the sun come up than it went back down. Would she be stuck lost and alone out here? And what of the dogs?

Her toes grew cold despite her fancy new boots from Lowood's in town. She had no idea how the dogs not only did it, but loved it.

Just as she was about to give up and call Shane, a four-wheeler approached head-on, slowing to a stop just a few yards ahead of her. "Hop on," the man said, and she happily complied. He mumbled something back over his shoulder, but she was so cold and so tired she couldn't make out the words. Instead, she just cozied into the welcome warmth of her rescuer's body.

A few minutes later, they were back at the starting line, and Lauren spied her whole team tied up outside the truck. A few other teams were also tied off as their mushers recapped the runs they'd just completed.

"Th-thank you," Lauren mumbled, not wanting to move from the warmth of the kind stranger.

"Ain't nothing," the man said. "Happens to the best of us. Maybe not *the best* of us, but you get my meaning."

She smiled and accepted a metal thermos from another racer. The hot coffee woke her right back up, made her feel human again.

Both men watched her as she drank, chatting with each other and leaving her mostly to recover on her own. When she'd finished the full thermos, she thanked them again and asked the question that had weighed heavily on her mind for hours now. "You won't tell Shane about this, will you?"

The men laughed, and Lauren thought that one of the smaller ones might actually be a woman, but it was hard to tell with how bundled up everyone was, especially with the sun already part-way down.

"Your secret's safe with us, but you hang tight to that bar.

Yeah? You can't see when some bumps are coming and that'll throw you every time if you aren't ready."

"How did you know that's what happened?"

"It happens more than you might know to rookie racers. Most especially cheechakos."

"Wh—?" Lauren began to ask, but the woman stopped her with a hearty laugh.

"People outside of Alaska. Like you, I'd wager. Anyway, even the best mushers get tossed from time to time. Lucky for you, you came to this track, and when we saw your team coming in without you, we figured you might need a pickup."

"So they sent me out with the four-wheeler to go find ya before dark sets in," her rescuer chimed in.

"And the rest of us corralled your dogs, unhooked 'em, fed 'em. Look at 'em now, curled into happy little husky pucks, ready to go home and take a long rest."

Lauren glanced toward the dogs, who definitely appeared contented, much to her relief. But who was she kidding thinking she could beat Shane's time? She hadn't even managed to finish the track, let alone earn a good time. So much for racing being her blood. Lauren wondered if her father had ever been tossed from the sled, or for that matter, if Shane had. Despite what the other men had told her, it seemed unlikely that anyone besides her could make such a foolish mistake.

"There, there," the small racer, who was definitely a woman, said as she patted Lauren's shoulder with a mittened hand. "It's how you learn."

"Did you ever fall?" Lauren whispered, feeling more at ease with the woman racer than the larger mixed gender group.

"More than once." She winked, and Lauren smiled. "And I'll tell you something else as long as you promise not to let anyone know it's me who told you."

Lauren nodded and waited for the big reveal.

"Your boss? Shane?" Her eyes sparkled like the untouched snow at the edges of the field as she whispered, "He has, too."

"The snow machining accident, you mean?"

"Not just that. He's made every mistake there is to make. He's lucky he didn't get hurt before now. But you know what?"

Lauren took a deep breath to make space for whatever secret this woman could tell her. "What?"

"It's good for you, taking a tumble like that. If you're not willing to take some risks, you can never be good at it."

As the sun sank further toward the horizon, Lauren couldn't help but wonder if that same advice applied to life every bit as much as it applied to the art of racing.

CHAPTER 24

LAUREN MADE IT HOME PAST DINNERTIME DESPITE THEIR early start that morning. Shane was nowhere to be seen, so she grabbed a quick meal on her own and headed off to bed early, completely exhausted from the hectic day.

Before she drifted off to sleep, she debated whether to tell Shane what had happened at the track. If she couldn't be honest with him, then she couldn't expect him to ever tell her his hidden truths, either. She would tell him, and if he gave her a hard time, she'd point out that he had once made the same mistakes, too.

Having made up her mind, she was able to enter into a deep, exhausted slumber.

Lauren dreamed of camping that night—of stargazing and swimming, singing songs around the campfire and stuffing her face with gooey s'mores. Shane was there, as was her father. Even Briar Rose had come with them to the campsite and ran excited circles around them, pouncing and leaping at the flames but not getting burned.

They sang Lolly Winston's latest hit song, and Shane surprised her with his smooth, baritone voice. She'd never heard him sing before, but had no doubt that this was truly his singing voice—and it was beautiful.

He moved closer to her so that their hips were touching. His voice dropped to a whisper as he murmured the lyrics, his face just inches from hers.

Closer, closer.

She could feel the soft syllables caress her cheek. Any minute now he'd kiss her, and the entire world would change for both of them.

He'd be healed. She'd be healed. They'd take their first steps toward happily ever after, together hand in hand.

She leaned forward and closed her eyes, waiting for what came next...

But it was not what she'd expected. Briar Rose shrieked as she burst through the fire and leapt between them. The scene split in half like an old scrap of paper, and Lauren watched helplessly as her father, Shane, and Briar Rose drifted one way and she the other.

The woodsy scents of smoke and earth lingered, filling her nostrils until she felt strained for breath. Briar Rose continued to bark, whine, howl, and screech.

Only it wasn't just Briar.

All the dogs were there now. And though she could no longer see them in her dream, their whimpering reached a fever pitch, an alarm that woke her from her sleep.

She sat up with a start. Was she dreaming? Or...?

The dogs continued their desperate cries from outside. The air still smelled of smoke, but the campsite was nowhere to be seen. Lauren sat alone in her bedroom, confused and scared.

Then her senses returned, and she finally understood what was happening.

"Fire!" she screamed, tugging on her boots and coats and flying toward the yard. She had to do something. She was the one who could move quickly. She needed to save Shane and the dogs before it was too late.

The dogs strained against their kennels, their eyes fixed on the source of the fire.

The garden shed stood partially ensconced in flames lapping tall and bright against the night sky. And she ran toward it, grabbing a discarded snow hook near the kennels, then returned to the fastest sprint she could manage.

Shane yelled something from behind her, but she didn't have time to make out the words. All her energy went toward moving her feet ever forward against the cold. Until it wasn't cold at all, and the heat of the flames brought beads of sweat to her brow.

Crash!

She knocked the heavy metal hook through each of the windows and reached through the broken glass to turn the knob from the inside. Luckily, the lock only kept people out, and she was able to turn it easily from the other side.

Having at last gained entry to the forbidden structure, her eyes darted toward the source of the fire. Curtains that had been singed to bits, pink, floral wallpaper obscured by soot, and plastic storage containers had melted, unable to protect the contents kept within.

What was this place?

No time to figure it out. She needed to extinguish the flames somehow. Would the hose reach all the way over here? Only one way to know for sure.

She was running again, and as she did, she passed Shane limping toward the shack with a fire extinguisher held clumsily in his hands.

They reconnected, she with her fire-fighting method and he with his. Together, they put out the flames and managed to save a small bit of the treasures inside.

Lauren turned toward Shane, not knowing what to say. She'd spied enough of the secret place to finally understand. He'd lost someone important to him, a woman, and this was his shrine to her memory.

No wonder he kept people out. He'd been hurt in the worst possible way, and now the little he had left of this lost love had vanished into the night. She nearly cried on his behalf, but no... He needed her to be strong, a source of comfort in this impossible situation.

For he likely felt as if he'd lost his loved one all over again, and now nothing could ever bring her back.

Lauren reached her arms around Shane, but he didn't return the hug. His body was rigid. Not even a tremor vibrated through his hands and arms, as it often did when he felt stressed.

Everything around them went still. Even the dogs quieted now.

"What did you do?" he said flatly. "*What did you do?*" he repeated it again and again, each time eerily devoid of emotion.

He still didn't trust her.

CHAPTER 25

LAUREN JERKED AWAY, SHOCKED THAT HE WOULD BLAME HER for the fire. "No, I woke up and it was... No, I didn't do this." She had a hard time defending herself. The act was indefensible, but it was not one she had committed. Who would do such a horrible thing, and least of all to a friend?

"You weren't supposed to go in there," he said, staring straight ahead at the charred remains of his once secret place.

"Shane, are you serious right now? *It was on fire.* If I didn't do something, it could've spread to the house or the kennels. Is your secret really more important than our lives? The dogs' lives?"

He shook his head for longer than was natural of such a gesture, saying nothing, staring straight ahead but seeing nothing. At last he murmured, "You started the fire. There was no one else. No one else could have, and you've always been nosing around my business. You couldn't pick the lock, so you set it on fire. Maybe you were frustrated with me. Maybe it was the only way you could get inside, but you did it. *You*."

Lauren felt as if she'd been punched in the face, and honestly, she wished he would hit her. It would hurt less, and it would make what needed to happen next that much easier. "Listen to yourself! That's crazy!" she cried. "I would never do this. Shane, I'm your friend, remember?"

He laughed bitterly. "Some friend you are. I should've sent you back when I had the chance, but no. I thought it could work out. I thought I should give you a chance, and now the only part I had left of her is gone. It's gone, Lauren! You took it, you took *her* away from me!"

She stepped backward, her chest heaving as she struggled under the weight of his accusation. "No, no, it's not like that. I don't even know who she is. I would never hurt you, Shane. Never." How silly she'd been, assuming he could return her feelings. He could never love her because he still carried a torch for some ghost. That was obvious now, and if she'd done a better job reading the clues, it would have been obvious sooner, too.

"Stop talking to me like you understand." His voice grew

distant as he crept into the damaged shed and examined what little remained. "You could never understand," he said as she joined him.

"Maybe I could if you opened up to me. I want to help." She placed a placating hand on his arm, but he ripped himself away from her touch.

"What a way you have of showing it," Shane sneered.

"I lost someone important to me, too. My father, he—"

"This isn't the same," Shane snapped. "You have no idea what you've done."

"Then tell me," she said gently, observing the shed's contents more closely now. Everything in the front was covered in soot and ash, but toward the back, a few bins remained unscathed. They held what looked like bolts of fabric—clothes maybe, most of them pink. She couldn't figure out any of the other items without stooping down to take a closer look, and she knew Shane wouldn't want her to do that. She stayed at his side, waiting for him to take back the hurtful accusation, to explain.

Something. Anything.

His voice sounded hoarse now as if it were single-handedly holding back a dam of tears. "You want me to tell you? Is that what you want?"

She looked over to him, but he continued to stare blankly ahead. She wanted to wrap him in her arms, to take away all the pain, but only if he would let her. He needed to let her help him. They could move past their losses together. "Yes, I'm here for you. I care about you, Shane. I want to help."

"Nobody asked you to do that." His eyes scanned the shed again, and when they landed on her, he grimaced and paced back out into the open yard.

Lauren followed him a step behind. They couldn't just act like this hadn't happened. He couldn't continue to disguise his hurt, to let it fester in his heart.

"I told you to stay away," he grumbled. "Play with fire and you'll get burned. Isn't that how the saying goes? But you couldn't stop there. You had to burn me, too. It's all ruined." He choked back a sob and, rather than continuing forward, fell to his knees in the snow, screaming in pain as he made contact with the ground.

"Is that what you really want?" she asked as she retrieved the crutches and tried to help him up.

He bullishly refused her, and it felt as if he were rejecting her for the first time all over again. As if they hadn't shared a single special moment, a single happy time. "That's what I want."

"Then I'll go, but please let me help you back inside first. Please let me make sure the dogs are okay."

"You'll go. And never come back." His words could have

been a question or a command, Lauren didn't know. All she knew is how much this hurt.

Now it was she who cried into the night air. "I promise," she said, turning her back to Shane Ramsey and walking away into the unknown.

CHAPTER 26

Lauren locked herself in her bedroom while trying to figure out what she would do next. She'd already sold her father's house, broken her apartment lease, quit her job, and left everything she'd had in New York behind to start anew in Alaska. Some good that had done.

Now her job and home had been pulled out from under her again, and other than the small inheritance her father had left her, she had nothing.

She hated calling on her friends in the middle of the night, but it seemed unlikely she could catch a cab at this hour, and she just needed to be gone before Shane could hurt her any more than he already had.

In the wake of their fallout, she had only one friend remaining in the whole state: Scarlett.

They'd exchanged a few texts and gone out for dinner a

couple times, but their friendship hadn't been fully cemented yet. Lauren hoped her new friend would forgive her the imposition of a midnight call for help, because she truly had no other option.

"Of course I'll come get you," the librarian said almost before Lauren even had to ask. "Text me the address, and I'll leave in five."

When Scarlett arrived, Lauren slipped out from her room, praying she wouldn't run into Shane as she made her great escape. But he'd already taken his car and left for some unknown place.

"What happened?" Scarlett asked, staring out at the burnt shed.

"Fire," Lauren answered, rubbing her hands together for warmth.

"Yeah, but how?" Scarlett's eyes were wide as if she opened them far enough, she could see all the answers.

"I don't know, but he thinks I did it."

"*You?* That's crazy."

Lauren felt the tears come back, and Scarlett must have noticed because she wrapped her friend into a tight, sisterly hug. "It's not your fault," she whispered into Lauren's hair. "Shane Ramsey became a monster after he lost his wife and daughter. Everyone says so. Sure, they all put up with him, because he's great at what he does, but nobody likes being around him anymore. He treat—"

"Wait." Lauren pulled back to study Scarlett's face, which was mottled with red from the cold air. "What did you just say?"

"Nobody likes Shane anymore," she said matter-of-factly and with a small shrug.

"About the... the wife and d-daughter?" Lauren didn't know if the cold was causing her stutter or if it was something more, something to do with her feelings for Shane.

Scarlett waved a hand dismissively. "Oh, I thought you knew about that. Have you really been living with the guy for over a month without learning anything about him?"

"Believe me, I've tried, but he's so closed off most of the time."

"Well, I don't know the particulars. Just that it was a nasty divorce, and after that, Shane always had a chip on his shoulder and meanness in his heart."

"What about his daughter?" Lauren ventured, still in shock over this big reveal.

"I don't know for sure. People say he was deemed an unfit father and lost custody."

"*Poor Shane*," Lauren said as his sad face swum into the vision of her memory. If only he'd told her. If only.

Scarlett seemed to feel differently about it, though. "It sucks, but it doesn't give him the right to take it out on the world. He made his own mistakes, and now he's living with the consequences. None of what happened is your fault."

"I know, but—"

"But nothing. Him kicking you out in the middle of the night is totally unacceptable. I always liked to think the rumors were exaggerated. I mean, how can anyone so good-looking on the outside be so ugly on the inside?"

Lauren shook her head, at a loss for words. How she wished Shane would have just told her all this himself. She could have reassured him that he was a good person, that sometimes life threw you a curve ball, but it didn't mean you were out of the game.

"Anyway," Scarlett said, "let's get out of here. Put this whole thing behind you. You can stay with me as long as you'd like, of course."

Lauren let out her breath in little puffs, refusing to cry, refusing to wonder what could have happened if things were different. She turned to her friend. "Thank you, I really appreciate that."

"Hey, it's what friends do." Scarlett put her arm over Lauren's shoulders as they walked to her car that idled in the driveway.

Lauren looked back toward the cabin one last time. This simple wooded structure had once held her hopes, dreams, even the sweet buds of love. She'd foolishly assumed this backdrop could serve as the setting to her forever, but now she realized her affection for Shane had always been one-sided.

Simply put, she loved him, because there wasn't anyone else to love in this isolated place. No, her feelings hadn't been real, and *his* had only been alive in her foolish, naive imagination. It was good—right—to leave.

She silently got into the car and refused to watch as Scarlett backed up and drove her far, far away from Shane Ramsey and hopefully from her feelings toward him as well.

CHAPTER 27

By the time Lauren woke up the next day, Scarlett had already left for work. She found this out by way of the bright yellow sticky note pinned to the cork board by the fridge.

At work. See you tonight, roomie!

XOX

Scar

Lauren checked the clock on the microwave. Nearly one o'clock in the afternoon here meant that, due to the four-hour time difference, her friends back in New York would just now be getting off from work. Should she call Joanna

Brocklehurst to beg for her old data entry job back? Or would it be better if Lauren closed her eyes and pointed to a random spot on the map, then headed there to start her new life... for a second time.

She had enough money from the sale of her father's house to pick up and start over, but was it what she wanted?

For that matter, what would her father do in this situation? Indeed, he had found himself in a similar place back when Lauren was little. He'd picked them up and moved them to their life in New York without a word of their former life in Alaska, but he'd also hung on to all these old articles and other mementos for years.

Did he regret that decision? Would she regret making a similar one?

She had to figure this out—and quickly. She hated to impose on Scarlett's kindness for any longer than necessary. Maybe one of her old high school friends could give Lauren a couch to crash on while she worked out the details on moving to a new city, new state, new Lauren.

Scrolling through her contacts, she searched for the friend most likely to be able and willing to help. Many of her classmates had stayed in their hometown, and most of them had even gotten married and started families of their own. They'd plotted their entire lives' courses, while Lauren didn't even know where she'd be for her next chapter.

Feeling like a complete failure, she decided to call her old friend, Helen, who had been their student body president during their junior and senior years. Helen would have the means to help along with plenty of advice. Maybe Lauren should just hand over control of her life to someone better suited. Someone like Helen.

Her friend answered after a few long, painful rings.

"Helen, it's me, Lauren."

"Hey, Laur." Helen sounded distracted, but didn't let on as to why. "I heard about your father. I'm so sorry. I wanted to be at the funeral, but I was in Paris for an internship and I just couldn't make it back with such short notice. I hope you understand."

"That's okay," Lauren reassured her, hoping that she didn't feel so guilty she'd refuse to offer any help now. "*Really*. I was so messed up I wouldn't have remembered seeing you there anyway."

"So what's going on now? I stopped by your house only to find you sold it in a hurry. Oh, by the way, the new neighbors there—well, I guess they're not your neighbors, are they?—the new people who live there, they gave me some of the mail that's come for you and your father. There's a lot of it. A package, too. Haven't you given a forward address to the post office yet?" Helen's voice dripped with condescension. Ahh, yes, that was why Lauren hadn't kept better touch with her after graduation.

"Shoot, I left in such a hurry, I didn't even think to do that."

"It's quite all right. I can send everything your way. Give me your address?"

Talking to Helen gave Lauren the clarity she needed, but not the solution she expected. Now she knew there would be no going back, only going forward. New York wasn't her home anymore, but she could still give Anchorage a chance.

She rummaged through the mail on Scarlett's desk until she found an envelope with her friend's address scrawled on the front. "I'm not sure how long I'll be here, but if I move, my friend can get everything to me," she explained before carefully reciting the address for Helen.

"It's like post office hot potato," Helen quipped. "What are you doing all the way up in Alaska?"

"I don't know," Lauren answered honestly. "But I'm going to figure it out soon enough."

"Well, call if you need anything else, okay?" She wondered if her friend really meant that and prayed she wouldn't be forced to find out later.

"I will," Lauren promised, and the two old friends said goodbye.

No sooner had she ended the call then a new voicemail notification popped up on her phone. She didn't recognize the number but could tell it was local because of the Alaskan state area code.

Lauren put her phone on speaker and clicked *play*.

"Hello, Lauren," a vaguely familiar woman's voice greeted her. "This is Mr. Ramsey's neighbor, Mary Fairbanks. We met a couple months ago? Anyway, Mr. Ramsey has asked me to give you a call and get your new address. He wants to send you a check for your pay. I have it right here." There was a rustling of papers as Mary paused. "It's a sizable amount, so you'll definitely be wanting it. Mr. Ramsey said it was unfortunate that he needed to let you go, but he wanted to make sure you were paid for the whole year."

Mary took a deep breath before continuing. "I don't know what you did to the man, but he's even more ornery than usual today. Called me at the crack of dawn, insisting I come over and help tend to the dogs. He's lucky I'm retired, or he'd be clear out of luck. It's not my place to judge, dear, but I think it's generally customary to provide two weeks' notice. Anyway, call me back so we can get this whole thing sorted."

Lauren listened as the woman rattled off her phone number and then hung up the phone. She'd call her back later, when it was less likely she'd have to speak to Mary instead of her voicemail program.

She understood why Shane hadn't called himself but wished he had.

CHAPTER 28

"Can I keep you forever?" Scarlett asked with a laugh before taking a big bite of the salmon Lauren had prepared for their dinner that night.

Scarlett's eyes grew wide as the flavors hit her tongue. "I mean it," she gushed, using her hand to cover her mouth so she could talk and eat at the same time. "I *am* keeping you, whether you like it or not."

"Sure, you can keep me, but I kind of need a job," Lauren answered with a huge smile.

"What's so wrong with being my stay-at-home room-mate? I almost never get to eat like this unless I visit my parents in the lower forty-eight."

Lauren rolled her eyes but secretly loved that Scarlett already found her indispensable. She hadn't managed that with Shane in more than a month, but somehow, it had taken less than a day with her new roomie. Isn't this the way things were *supposed to* be?

"You know..." Scarlett dragged a spoonful of aioli across her salmon filet, slathering the entire surface as she chattered on. "I'm sure we could find you something at the library."

"Me? A librarian?" Lauren's voice squeaked with excitement at this idea. "That would be super cool."

"Not exactly." Scarlett took a quick sip of water before continuing. "I mean, you need a master's degree in library sciences for that, but you said you studied English, right?"

Lauren nodded, eager to hear more.

Scarlett bobbed her head as if in agreement with herself. "*Yeah.* Yeah, we'll manage something. Or, maybe I could introduce you around U of A, see if any of the professors need a research assistant."

"Why are you so amazing?"

Scarlett flushed. "Me? No. Actually, *you're* the most exciting thing that's happened to me in years."

"*I* am?"

Scarlett nodded so vigorously that she choked on her rice pilaf. She banged on her chest, coughed, and then continued eating. Lauren wished she could eat the way her new friend did and remain stick thin. Lauren had never been a stick and, these days, she was downright Amazonian with all the extra muscle she'd put on running Shane's dogs.

Scarlett took a few long gulps of water before explaining. "So I grew up in Texas, a tiny town world famous for its apples. Anyway, I'd always known I wanted to be a librarian, so I went where they had a job for me."

"To Loussac?" Lauren said, recalling their first meeting over the microfiche.

"To Loussac. And right away, I knew I'd found my home. I fell in love with everything about this place—the nature, the people, the history, and especially the Iditarod."

Lauren shook her head in awe. "How old are you, Scar? You can't be much older than me, and I'm just twenty-five."

Scarlett waggled four fingers at Lauren. "I'll be thirty next year. But, anyway, that's not the point. The point, is I fell in love with dog racing every bit as much as I've always loved my books. I read about it, studied it, watched it, but I never in my wildest dreams ever thought I could actually maybe do it for myself. That is, until you came along."

Lauren laughed in disbelief. "What did I do?"

"You were just *you*, Lauren, and that was enough. You came to the library that day, coming to the sport with no background, working for one of the most infamous men in the business, and when you told me you did it all on a whim? You blew my mind a little."

"I did?"

"You did. I've always planned and plotted my life so carefully, done the things you're supposed to do, not necessarily the things I wanted to do. But then, I thought, *she's* doing it, so why can't you do it, too?"

Lauren glanced around the small apartment which housed a noticeable absence of dogs.

"Oh no. Not yet. A tiger can't change its stripes overnight, but I did put in for a sabbatical, so that maybe next season, I can..." She blushed and set her fork down beside the empty place. "I can be a musher, too. You inspired me to follow my dreams, and that makes you my favorite person in basically the whole wide world."

"I'm not part of that world anymore. Shane fired me. Well, I kind of quit, kind of got fired. Point is, it's not what I'm doing any longer."

"But your father..." Scarlett blushed and the color overtook her entire face. "It's who you are," she finished.

Lauren sighed. "I'm starting to wonder if I really knew my father at all. He kept such a big part of himself hidden from me, and I'm no closer to learning why he quit or why he kept this huge secret for so many years."

Scarlett carried their plates to the sink and began to scrub at the dishes. "Well, tell you what. As much as I love having you stay home and cook for me, come to the library with me tomorrow. I'll set you up with some more research materials, and you can have the whole day to learn more about your family's history. The answers are out there. You just have to keep looking, and I'll help, too."

"Scarlett, that's so nice. Thank you."

"Hey, no need to thank me. It's what friends do. Yeah?"

"Yeah," Lauren said, returning the fist bump Scarlett offered. So this is what it felt like to be wanted, accepted, and appreciated. None of these were things she'd felt while living with Shane—at least, not for longer than a few moments at a time.

Being here with Scarlett was right. She'd made a friend for life. The rest would come in time.

CHAPTER 29

LAUREN LEFT THE LIBRARY THE FOLLOWING AFTERNOON having learned many things. She'd learned that Iditarod was named for the Ingalik word Halditarod, which meant "distant place," and that the most winning musher of all time was Rick Swenson, whose fifth and final victory had taken place in 1991—meaning, Lauren supposed, that her father had raced against him at one time. She knew that in the early 90's, people were proud of their mullets and high tops.

But what she hadn't learned was anything new about her father.

Scarlett invited her back for the following day, but the more Lauren researched without uncovering any additional clues, the more it felt like she would never know the man her father had been—not during his racing years, and not in the years since.

The betrayal stung anew. She'd confided her first crush in him, told him schoolyard secrets she otherwise only entrusted to her Lisa Frank diary, even confessed when she'd stolen the fancy feather pen from Heather McEntyre's desk. But he'd kept years of his life from her.

Years!

Did the secret-keeping stop when he'd left the sport, or had he hidden other things as well? Her father could have been living a dual life for all she knew, and here he'd been her entire life and world.

"Chin up," Scarlett said as she pulled into the carport. "We'll figure out what happened. I promise."

"We?" Lauren asked with a sniff.

"Of course, we. You think I would leave you alone in this? *No way.* Let me use my librarian super powers to help you find the truth. I can get you more books, more primary sources, even normally off-limit stuff." Her friend squealed as she unbuckled her seatbelt and opened the door. "Oh, it's going to be so much fun!"

Lauren felt her tears turn to laughter as she followed Scarlett back into the apartment building.

"Books, and databases, and microfiche, oh my!" Scarlett sang as she linked her arm in Lauren's. "We're off to discover the secrets, the surprising secrets of... Lauren's dad."

More laughter rang out as the two women skipped up

the stairs, still arm and arm, and Scarlett continued her *Wizard of Oz* parody. "We hear he was a—Oh, hello!"

Being taller than Lauren, Scarlett spotted the figure sitting on the floor outside their door a second before her friend as the two climbed the stairs. There, pushed back against the wall with his crutches propped neatly beside him, sat her former employer, Shane Ramsey. He lifted his chin and widened his eyes as the women approached, but neither smiled nor frowned, hiding his true feelings just as well as ever.

"I'll just go get started on dinner," Scarlett said, letting herself into the apartment and gently shutting the door behind her.

"What are you doing here?" Lauren remained standing because it felt like it gave her more control of the situation, that at any moment she could make a run for it if she needed.

"Come home, Lauren," he said. "I made a mistake. *I need you.*"

She wasn't sure which part was nicer to hear—or which made her angrier.

"We can't keep doing this," she said, crossing her arms and staring down at him with the coldest expression she could muster. "You're yanking me around like I'm some kind of toy. It's not right."

"I know. I'm so sorry. You deserve better than that."

She took a deep breath and tried to relax her posture. Did he really mean those words? Would things be different from here on out? "You're right. I do."

"And I'm going to do better, I promise. Only, please come home, Lauren. Please."

"How can I trust you when you don't trust me? You go to these ridiculous lengths to protect your secret past, and then you accuse me of burning down your shed. Intentionally, no less."

"I know, I know." His voice cracked, and he hung his head.

Lauren thought she may have spied the beginnings of tears, but Shane quickly hid his face in his hands and rubbed them away.

"I'm not used to it. That's not an excuse, but it's the truth, the first of many I came to tell you if you're willing to hear them."

She didn't know which question to start with. *Not used to what? What other truths did you come to say? Does this mean you do care about me after all?* She sank to the floor beside him, deciding to let him start wherever he needed to. "Go ahead. I'm listening."

His hand twitched toward hers, but then he pulled it away and set it on his injured knee. He looked straight ahead at the stairwell as he spoke. "People don't like me, and they haven't for a long time. I don't know why you're different, but for whatever reason, you put up with my temper. You help make me feel happy, and not just because you're great with the dogs. You stand up to me. You challenge me. You make me laugh, and you make me the best dinners I've had in ages. Which I also miss, by the way."

He laughed softly, but it got stuck in his throat on the way out. He looked to her as if he wanted her to say something more, but she needed to hear more if she were really, truly going to forgive him for everything that happened two nights before, everything that had happened since they first met that January day outside his kennels.

"I..." He started again but faltered, swallowing back an apparent lump in his throat. "I want to be honest with you, because *you're right*. We are friends, and I do care about you. I didn't want to, but it's too late to change that now."

"Go on," Lauren urged in a whisper.

"I hid my past from myself, too, Lauren. Yes, I have—had—the shed filled with her things, but I almost never go out there. That night, after the tavern with my old buddies, I was missing her so much, so I did. I had to see the shed to feel better. They asked me questions, talked about what had happened, because they all knew. The mushing community isn't as big as you might think. Everyone knows everything about everybody. I think that's part of why I began enjoying having you around so much. It was like a fresh start. You didn't know, and I felt like if you found out, you'd hate me just as much as I hate myself."

He stopped again, cleared his throat, looked to her as if begging to not have to say more. But she needed to hear this, and she could tell he needed to say it, too.

Lauren placed a hand on his shoulder, hoping it would give him the courage he needed to go forward.

Another deep breath. "Three years ago, I had a wife and a daughter, but I never made them a priority and I didn't deserve them. I was always thinking about the dogs, working them, running any race that would take me. I was one of the best, but I had to be *the* best. And that takes a huge time commitment. I gave the sport my everything, which meant there was nothing left for my family."

He choked on a sob again, but this time, he let the tears cascade down his cheeks. "I wasn't surprised when my wife left me, but I hadn't expected for her to be so angry, to seek revenge like she did."

Shane turned to look at her. His normally stormy eyes shone clear and bright. "She took my daughter, too. She did everything she had to... to make sure I lost custody, to make sure I was out of both of their lives for good. And I haven't seen my little girl since. I've been living three years now without my heart, but the place where it's supposed to be still aches so much."

Lauren laid her head on his shoulder. It was a tender

gesture, an intimate one, but it also felt right. "Thank you for telling me," she said. "All I ever wanted was for you to be honest with me, to let me in."

He rested his head against hers, and they sat in silence until their individual rhythms synchronized. His heart, her breath, moved as one harmony.

"Will you come home?" he asked at last.

"I will," she said. More and more, home had begun to feel like a person instead of a place. Would he one day feel the same about her, too?

Tonight was a start.

CHAPTER 30

HER NAME WAS ROSIE, AND SHE HAD JUST TURNED FOUR years old when Shane saw her last. Shane filled Lauren in on the details as he drove her back home to the cabin that night.

"I don't know where she is or even what her last name is anymore," he explained, the words seeming to come easier as each new truth was revealed. "For all I know, Isabel could have changed it on me."

"But now that I know, I can help," Lauren pointed out. "I can help you find her again."

"What makes you think she'd even want to see me, or remember me, for that matter? She was so little, and I failed her. No, I deserve what I got." He used the buttons on his steering wheel to flick on the radio, but Lauren reached forward and shut it off.

"No, you really don't deserve any of this. You're a good

man, Shane. And, trust me, your daughter will want to see you. My dad kept a huge part of his life from me, but I would give anything to have him back even if only for a day. Girls need their fathers. Rosie needs you, just as much as you need her."

"But how can I get her back, Lauren? It's impossible."

"I don't know yet, but we'll figure it out." She reached over to clasp his shaking hand in hers. "Together."

They drove in companionable silence for a while as Lauren worked the various tidbits she'd discovered about Shane into this narrative. The old court summons must have somehow pertained to the divorce or the custody hearing. His temper and intense commitment to the dogs were also likely tied to what had happened with his ex-wife. Shane mentioned having been in the shed the night of the fire, so it was quite likely he'd left a space heater on or a candle unsnuffed—either of which could have easily caused a spark.

There were still a couple things she couldn't reconcile, but maybe now he'd be willing to tell her.

"Shane?" she ventured.

"Hmm?" Just like that, some of the tension returned. It would take time until he was fully comfortable, if he ever got there with her. She hoped that one day he would.

Since she'd already disrupted his calm, she went ahead with the first of her questions. "Why did you name your dog after your daughter?"

"Briar Rose?" He laughed. This seemed to be an easy question at least. "I didn't name her. Rosie did."

Lauren chuckled, too. "After herself?"

"Well, she was two at the time, and wanted a dog of her own. When we asked what she wanted to name her new pet, she had exactly three suggestions: *Doggie*, *Poopie*, or *Rosie*. So we compromised and named her Briar Rose and eventually switched to just calling her Briar." His eyes seemed to glaze over from the memory, as if he was watching it play out before him as they drove.

Lauren laughed again. "Sounds like my kind of kid. But then why didn't Briar go with Rosie when she moved out?"

"That dog loved my little girl, and my little girl loved her. I know they would have liked to be together, but Isabel didn't want any part of my world left in hers." He leaned back into the bucket seat as if all his energy had suddenly been sucked clean away. "I always hoped she'd change her mind and come back for Briar," His voice grew shaky again. "But after months passed, I realized it wasn't going to happen. I couldn't stand having the dog around the house whimpering waiting for her little human to come home. It reminded me how much I missed my girl, too, so eventually I decided to put Briar Rose outside with the others, and that's where she's been ever since."

So that's why Briar Rose was so different!

She wasn't even a sled dog. It also explained why Lauren

had instantly bonded with the former pet. They were both looking for someone to love after losing the person they each loved most in the world. "Can I ask one more question?"

"Shoot," he said. She hated to keep asking him to relive these painful moments, but at the same time, she knew it would be easier for the both of them to get it all out at once.

"Why do you have all those nice suits in your closet but then never wear them?" She glanced toward him just in time to see him smile. Another easy question. That was good.

"I knew you were snooping through my closet that day." He smirked but didn't seem angry. "Sometimes I wear them for endorsement deals. You have to understand that up here, mushers are a bit like celebrities. I do make prize money whenever I win or place high enough in the bigger races, but most of my earnings come from these types of deals. I haven't had any since my injury, though."

"What else?" Lauren asked.

"What do you mean what else?"

"You said sometimes you wear them for that reason, implying that there are other times and other reasons."

"Okay, Nancy Drew." He laughed, and she joined him. "Of course, I can't get anything past you."

"Well?" she asked when he didn't continue on his own.

"I have some family money." He shrugged as if it wasn't any big deal. "Honestly, I think it's part of why Isabel fell for me in the first place. She liked my money more than she ever liked me, and she never agreed with my decision to walk away from the business and take up mushing instead."

"What kind of business?" Lauren pried, unable to picture Shane doing anything other than running those dogs.

His lip curled into a sneer as he spat, "Big oil."

She must have worn a look of disgust across her face, too, because Shane said, "Yeah, exactly. It never felt right, and I figured just because I was born into it didn't mean I had to live out my entire life there."

"So you quit?" she supplied.

"I quit, and let my brothers and sister fight it out without me."

"And Isabel didn't approve of that situation?"

"Heck no. She thought she was marrying one of Alaska's wealthiest heirs, and thought me walking away meant I didn't love her or our daughter, that I didn't care about providing a future."

"But that's crazy!" Lauren argued on his behalf.

"I can understand where she was coming from, though." He shrugged again. "She married with the assumption that our life would go one way, and suddenly I zigzagged another. The thing is, I still make pretty good money and a comfortable living. Only now I can live with myself over it."

"Can you, though? You're always so mopey and angry."

"Yeah, but not about that."

She glanced toward him again and watched as his features crumpled into a mask of sadness. This poor man had lost so much, and he thought he deserved it, too. How long would he have to atone for his sins before he could find peace again? Lauren would make sure it was the shortest period of time possible. She would help deliver him from his guilt, his grief, his loss, because he didn't feel he was worthy of fighting for himself.

"We're going to find her, Shane," she promised. "You have my word."

CHAPTER 31

STEPPING BACK INTO THE CABIN AT 1847 THORNFIELD WAY truly felt like coming home.

"I made some changes while you were gone," Shane said as he hobbled in after her. "Not as many as I'd like, though. Knees kept slowing me down."

Lauren glanced around the living room, which still looked much the same to her. "Is there something I can help with?"

"Yes. Tomorrow, though. I barely slept the last two nights, and considering how exhausted I am, we're lucky I managed to get us back in one piece."

She stepped deeper into the room and noticed the carpet had been vacuumed, maybe even washed. Turning back toward Shane with a goofy smile on her face, she said, "Didn't sleep, huh? Does that mean you missed me?"

He crossed his arms over the crutches. "Haven't I opened up enough for one night?"

She raised an eyebrow at him, and he laughed.

"You know I did. That's why I came to get you back," he said through a smile.

She gave him a quick hug. "It's just nice to hear, is all."

Shane let out a monster-sized yawn, trying and failing to speak through it. "I... very... know."

"Fine, fine. Go to bed. I'll see you in the morning."

As much as Lauren looked forward to seeing the dogs again, she, too, craved a good night's rest after two nights tossing and turning on Scarlett's sofa. Back at home now, she slept like a rock or a log or something else that doesn't move very much, snoozing straight through to morning when the smell of freshly fried bacon wafted into her room.

"Rise and shine!" Shane crowed from the doorway, where he stood with a precariously balanced tray of eggs, bacon, and orange juice, waiting for her permission to enter.

"What's all this?" she asked, rubbing sleep from her eyes while hoping he couldn't smell her morning breath from where he stood.

"Me making an effort to be a better friend, especially since I have a pretty big favor to ask you."

"That favor must be huge," she mused. "Are you going to have some breakfast, too?"

"Believe me, I already did. There was at least four times this amount of bacon when I got started."

"Well, have a seat." Lauren pulled her legs into a crossed position and invited him to sit at the foot of the bed, then took a huge gulp of orange juice to hopefully sweeten her breath. "What can I do you for?"

Shane took a dramatic sigh. So she was getting breakfast and a show. Not a bad way to start the morning.

"I don't know if you've ever noticed this," he whispered as if confiding a secret. "But the house is kind of messy."

"No! Really?" She rolled her eyes before taking a huge bite of scrambled eggs.

"Always so funny, even first thing in the morning," he said with a sarcastic chuckle. "The fire in the shed was kind of a wakeup call. By the way, the fire marshal told me it was an electrical fire. Turns out I left the space heater on and it caught the curtains."

"I figured that out, but good to hear you admit it."

"Nothing gets by you, does it?"

"Nope," she said before biting clean into a crispy strip of bacon.

"You know how sorry I am about that, but it's actually good it happened."

"Oh?"

"Yeah, the wakeup call," he reminded her. "But not a nice one like a good-looking friend serving you breakfast in bed."

She rolled her eyes again. "What kind of wakeup call, then?"

"The kind where I realized all this stuff isn't just a fire hazard, but an emotional one, too. If I can't clear out the clutter of the past, I'll never be able to move forward into the future."

This was the first time she'd heard him talk of a future outside of the context of mushing. Did this new future include her?

"You sound a bit like a fortune cookie, but I think I understand. You want me to help you clear out this mess, right?"

"If you wouldn't mind?" His voice cracked, which she found hysterical coming from her burly and bearded friend.

"Of course I'll help. On one condition." She stopped laughing and took another thoughtful bite from her eggs. "Actually, make that two." She sucked down the rest of her orange juice, knowing the waiting was driving him crazy—and liking that fact very much.

"Well? You going to make me wait until we both grow old?"

Now he made jokes about them growing old together? Interesting.

Lauren wagged her fork at him as she detailed her side of the deal. "The first condition is that you bring Briar Rose back inside. She's a pet, and she belongs in the house."

He nodded, briefly glancing toward the window as if he could see the kennels from here. "And the other?"

"Promise you'll help me find her."

"Briar Rose?"

Lauren sighed. "You know who I mean, Mr. Wise Guy."

"What if we can't?"

"We can."

"What if we—?"

"We will."

Shane stole her last piece of bacon, but she decided to let that slide. "How can you feel so confident?" he said.

"Because now you're not alone in this anymore. I don't know if you've noticed this, but I tend to dig my heels in when there's something I want."

Shane raised a hand to his chest in mock surprise. "No!" he cried.

"Yes, Mr. Wise Guy, and I want this as much as I want to learn the truth about my father. Maybe even more, because there's still time to make things right for the two of you."

She linked her fingers through his for a quick squeeze, but when she tried to pull away, he held tight.

"So," Shane said after a few charged moments, finally letting her hand go. "Is Mr. Wise Guy my new nickname, then?"

Lauren laughed. "That okay with you, Mr. Wise Guy?"

"I've got to admit, I'll miss you calling me Mr. Grump, but I'll take it. I'm just glad you're home."

CHAPTER 32

AFTER BREAKFAST, SHANE HELPED LAUREN WORK THE DOGS. He fed them and cleaned their kennels while she focused on exercising them. Shane's injury made him slow, but the little tips he offered Lauren as they worked helped her use the time more efficiently than ever. Finally, she was properly trained for the job she'd held just shy of six weeks.

After this shared morning routine, they turned to their new chore of tidying up the house and finishing demolition of the shed. As much as she could, Lauren searched for clues amidst the debris and clutter. Whenever she found something that might help her locate Shane's missing daughter, she committed the details to memory, including where they'd filed it or which rummage bag they'd relinquished it to.

She planned to snap pictures later that evening

while Shane slept. That way she could advance their search for Rosie while not forcing the girl's father to face the past any more than he wanted to. She was so proud of him for finally letting go of what had been and committing to finding *what could be.* Lauren vowed that she would do everything in her power to help the family reach a happy ending—even if that ending didn't include her.

Around six that evening, a knock sounded at the door. Lauren looked to Shane for an explanation, but he just shrugged off her quizzical expression and hobbled over to answer it.

A moment later, he was back with a tall paper bag full of something that smelled absolutely wonderful. "Ready for some dinner?" he asked as he carried the delivery toward the table. Right on cue, Lauren's stomach growled loudly enough for both of them to hear.

"I'm famished," she admitted, "but let me get Briar first. I'm sure she'd love to lie under the table and beg for scraps while we eat."

"Lauren..." he warned.

"Hey, I kept my end of the deal. Now you need to keep yours." She continued toward the door, unwilling to negotiate this point.

Shane called after her, "Don't give her any scraps, though. She hasn't had people food for years, and having it now could make her sick. Besides, this meal is supposed to be special. For us."

"You worry too much," Lauren teased before slamming the door behind her and racing out to the kennels to untie Briar Rose—whom she would now call just Briar, to avoid making Shane uncomfortable—and bring her inside.

"He says it's special," Lauren told the dog as she undid the latch on her lead. "What do you think that means?"

Briar howled and jumped up to give Lauren kisses the moment she was free, and Lauren couldn't help but wonder if those weren't the only kisses she might receive that evening. For try as she may, her feelings for Shane Ramsey refused to abandon her. Instead, they continued to grow rapidly. With each new confession of truth, each new kind gesture and friendly heckle, she found herself falling deeper and deeper under his spell.

Still, he'd been hurt—and badly. She cared too much for him to rush him into anything that would open the wounds of his broken heart before he was ready.

One day, perhaps, the timing would be right, and she'd just know.

And he'd know.

And they'd live happily ever after. The end...

Or something to that effect.

Today was not that day, could not be that day, because they still had so much to do, so many dragons to slay before declaring any type of victory. They'd start with finding his daughter, and then they'd find the truth about her father. Both mysteries needed to be resolved so that the pair of friends could heal and truly examine their futures, decide if those futures should intertwine.

Oh, she hoped it could work out for them.

Ultimately, though, Lauren's father had raised her to be a practical woman, with her head glued firmly to her shoulders rather than floating up in the clouds. As much as she loved to envision fairytale endings, life had already proven that it enjoyed writing a different kind of story for her.

Loss, guilt, grief, settling for what was more than striving for what could be. It was a tale as old as her time on this earth. It was why she'd settled for a job at data corp rather than taking the time to uncover her true passion, and it was probably why it had been so easy for her father to keep his past hidden from her all these years.

Not anymore, though.

Lauren finally knew what she wanted from life, and Shane had been a huge part of that, whether he'd tried to be or not.

When she and the red husky came back inside, they found Shane setting the table with china plates rather than the usual disposable ones. He'd even brought out a bottle of white wine she'd spied in the fridge earlier that day.

"What's all this?" she asked with a sly smile as Briar bolted through the doorway and pushed Shane back against the wall in a flurry of tail thumps that actually wagged her entire body.

"Easy, girl!" He laughed and stroked the dog's head.

"You talking to Briar or me?" Lauren quipped.

"Maybe both," he said, commanding the dog to sit with a quick hand gesture.

"What are we celebrating tonight?" Lauren asked, pointing her chin toward the chilled wine and elegant flatware. "Your fresh start?"

Shane crossed the kitchen to retrieve a bottle opener from the neat and tidy junk drawer, then came to stand right before her as he tossed the tool up and down in his palm. "Actually, we're celebrating *yours*."

"Mine?"

"Yep."

"Care to elaborate?"

"Nope."

She fixed him with a stern glare.

"Just kidding," he said with a chuckle. "Sit down and try the best halibut in the entire state of Alaska for yourself. I promise to explain everything."

She did as told, removing one of the takeout boxes from the large delivery bag and serving herself some of everything. "What is all this?" she asked, pulling out box after box from the bag, wondering why he'd ordered enough to feed ten people at least.

"It's from that little cafe in town, Maurice's. Everything is so good that that's what I ordered."

"Come again?"

"Everything. I ordered everything on the menu," he declared proudly as he opened another container and showed her what was inside. "Try the creamy stuff first. It's delicious."

Lauren popped a spoonful of the light, creamy dish into her mouth and immediately moaned with pleasure. "You weren't kidding. Except now I wonder if you ordered enough!"

Shane laughed as he transferred the various cuisines to his plate as well.

"Okay, so this is definitely how you celebrate," Lauren mumbled between bites. "Good food, good wine, good friends. Just need to know if we have a good cause."

"Of course we do. We're celebrating your official start as a musher." He raised his glass in toast, but she stared at him slack-jawed rather than return the gesture.

"Umm, hello, I've been doing this for almost two months now," she argued.

"You've been *a handler* for almost two months. Starting tomorrow, you're *a musher.*"

"Like a promotion?"

"Sure, if you want to think of it that way. I've signed you and the dogs up for your first race."

Oh, this was welcome news! She raised her glass at last and clinked it to Shane's. They both took sips of the sweet white wine and smiled across the table at each other.

"Is it the Iditarod?" she asked, apparently ruining the moment with her naivety.

"Are you kidding? No way. You don't jump straight to the big race, Lauren. You need time to really get your bearings before taking it all the way."

She frowned and set her fork down after finishing the entire serving of the gray dish she'd plopped onto her plate. "I don't know... Are you sure I can do this?"

"You mean because you fell off the sled and lost the dogs during your practice run?"

Her face turned beet red. At least, she assumed it did, because it felt like her cheeks were on fire from the embarrassment. "How did you—?"

He laughed again, and now she was certain she'd heard Shane laugh more that one day than all the rest of the time she'd known him. "Word travels fast. It's a small community, remember? Anyway, yes, falling off is almost like a rite of passage. Just like having your first race is an important rite for any new musher."

"You really think I can do it? That I can be good?"

"I know you can."

"Well, if Mr. Grump believes in me, then I believe in me, too."

They both laughed together.

"Back to Mr. Grump, I see?"

She shrugged. "Old habits die hard. Just promise me one thing."

"What's that?" He quirked an eyebrow at her.

"Please don't make me race against you anytime soon. Give me the chance to win one or two first, eh?"

Shane patted his leg and called Briar over to his side, then handed her a piece of fried, breaded moose meat, which the dog accepted with relish.

It was only after the dinner and wine were both polished off and the dishes had been cleaned and dried that Lauren realized he'd changed the topic.

CHAPTER 33

THE NEXT MORNING FOUND LAUREN HARD AT WORK, scrambling to follow Shane's instructions as he barked them into the cold pre-dawn air. Although he generally seemed happier in life now, it was easy to forget this change during his military-like training drills.

Lauren no longer ran the dogs alone, but with Shane in the basket of the sled, calling out adjustments she needed to make now and jotting down notes he planned to share with her later. Work no longer ended with the day, but now they discussed technique over dinner and well into the night. He even had her reading his old copy of Jack London.

At first she thought it might be overkill, but then she noted that the sled had more give when she used the techniques Shane had drilled into her. Whenever she tried to lean into a turn, the sled moved with her, like they were becoming one.

"With more give, there's less likelihood that you'll get bounced off when you lean into your turns. Just try not to get too low, or you'll squish me in here," Shane shouted from his new seat of honor inside the basket.

At the end of every day, the dogs would pant happily and curl into little fluff balls as they went to sleep, and Shane would down a few pills to deal with the pain rattling around in the sled caused.

Lauren tried to suggest that he didn't need to come on every run, but he shrugged off her concerns, showing up the next day with pillows.

"No chance of my squishing you now that you're bundled up like the Michelin man," she joked, but he did not laugh. The business of sledding was far too serious for him to ever laugh at the jokes she made out there.

As the days continued to pass in a productive blur, Shane wasn't the only one whose comfort was pushed to the limit. As soon as Lauren felt like she was getting used to a particular trick or technique, he would change the game on her. Once she'd managed a good time on one trail, he'd remove two of the dogs from her team and have her run it again, telling her she needed to manage the same time with the reduced team.

"Strength training," he called from the basket. "We

started with all of them pulling the two of us. We cut down slowly so they get used to pulling more. Normally we'd use the snow machine for this, but... well, you know."

When the lead dogs got used to her commands, he'd switch up the pair, sometimes even putting a team dog next to a normal lead dog.

At night, as they ate dinner, Shane would regale her with tales from the trails, as he called them. Times he'd fallen, times he'd had to use his body as a snow hook, even the time he'd gotten soaked falling into a lake during a summer run.

"One thing you've got going for you, Lauren, and it's going to make you a great musher: you know how to roll with the punches. Out there, nothing goes as planned," he said, tapping his knee with the cane he now used.

"Being able to adapt and move quickly will save you and your team. It's why I keep messing with your team setup. You can't rely on just a few dogs. If one gets hurt and you need to drop a dog at a checkpoint, you need to know how to adjust your team accordingly. It's just you and them out there. They depend on you just as much as you depend on them. That's why they're a team. You all are."

"*We* all are," Lauren said, shooting him a smile.

"I like the sound of that," he said before stuffing his mouth again.

CHAPTER 34

Lauren invited Scarlett up to Puffin Ridge for a ride on the sled. It would be her first time running with someone other than Shane in the basket, and no one deserved that honor more. Scarlett had been working hard toward the mysteries of Edward Dalton and Rose Ramsey, and Lauren wanted to make sure she was properly thanked.

Her guest came to the door bundled tightly in every possible article of winter wear and then some. She even wore hot pink snow pants, which made Lauren and Shane both laugh.

"Oh, I brought the mail your friend from the lower forty-eight sent up. It's on the front seat of my car. Should I go grab it?" Scarlett asked as she stomped the snow from her regulation-standard bunny boots, making it clear she'd done her research when it came to this sport.

Lauren gave her friend a hug hello. "Sure. Can you set it on the table, then meet me around back? I'll start prepping the sled."

"Have fun out there," Shane said as he settled into his recliner.

"Wait, you're not coming with us?"

"Don't need to. Besides, I'll only get in the way." He grimaced as he shifted in his chair and propped his cane on the arm.

"If you're sure…"

He waved her off. "I'm sure. Go get 'em, tiger."

She laughed and shook her head. Shane needed a serious slang update, but she'd work on that later. Right now, the excitement of having her friend at the cabin and running her first full team—she decided not to count the unfortunate time she'd fallen from the sled—were more than enough to hold her focus.

"Here I am!" Scarlett sang as she skipped through the snow and made her way over to the dogs. "I can't believe I'm here at Shane Ramsey's and going to take a ride with his team."

"Today," Lauren said, hooking Fred on, "they're my team."

"You know what I mean!" Scarlett looked back toward the house. Shane's silhouette was just visible through the large front window. "He seemed nice today. Are you two getting along better?"

Lauren felt heat rise to her cheeks and hoped her friend would attribute it to wind burn rather than embarrassment. "Yep. He's really turned over a new leaf."

Scarlett looked across the snowy valley. "Funny, I don't see any leaves anywhere."

"I love you to death, Scar, but maybe you should stop trying so hard to be funny."

Scarlett stuck out her tongue and then immediately drew it back in. "Ack, that's cold!"

Lauren finished securing the bungie cords and even added one of Shane's pillows to the basket for her friend. "You ready?"

"Darling, I was born ready."

They high-fived through their thick mittens.

Lauren couldn't tell who was more excited. "Then hop in the basket, and let's do this thing."

She pulled up the snow hook and shouted to the team, "Hike, hike!" Holding tight to the handlebar, she ran behind the sled, helping as the dogs got up to speed. With a quick hop and a stumble, she managed to wrestle her way back on to the footboards.

Scarlett oohed, ahhed, and even raised her hands in the air as if she were on a rollercoaster ride. Lauren loved every second of it.

After three hours, when the dogs were tuckered out and the cold had seeped deep into both of the girls' bones, Lauren directed them back toward the kennels so the two of them could get inside and get something hot in their stomachs.

"That was... ahh-mazing!" Scarlett cheered. "When can we do it again?"

Lauren laughed, thankful she had managed to make such a wonderful friend. "Soon, soon, I promise."

"What I don't get is how Shane ever gave this up. It's like flying, you know. Light gliding across the heavenly plane."

"Somebody's been hitting the purple prose hard, I see. And you know Shane had to stop for a little while because of his injury." She patted Fred on the head and told him what a good boy he was as she hooked him up to his house.

Scarlett helped tie up the other dogs, but Lauren still checked each latch, knowing how badly her friend would feel if a dog got loose because of her.

"But Lauren, how long has it been now?" Scarlett watched as the musher checked each dog, even those that hadn't been run that afternoon. "You've been here for three months, right?"

"Yeah. So?" She finished with Zeke and stomped back through the snow toward the cabin.

"So... What if he never gets better?"

Lauren shook her head. "No, you don't see how hard he

works at his physical therapy. You don't know how much he loves the sport."

"But I love it, too, and I'm not out there running my own team. Sometimes life doesn't give you what you want."

"Scar, please. Shane is going to get better, and if you ask him nicely, he may even give you an autograph."

Just like that, the mood lightened again as Scarlett asked, "Oooh, really? You think so?"

"There's only one way to find out. Let's go inside. I have a stew that's been slow cooking all day, and it has our names on it."

Still, Scarlett's words nagged at Lauren. Was she really so optimistic about Shane's recovery that she'd ignored certain signs?

No, impossible.

Shane was a fighter. Just like her. He would get better.

He had to.

CHAPTER 35

Lauren and Scarlett burst into the kitchen, still high from the thrill of the track. They found Shane standing in front of the counter with a look of displeasure on his face.

"Were we too loud?" Lauren asked, hoping he hadn't truly returned to his Mr. Grump ways.

He shook his head and pointed to the opened box on the counter.

Lauren followed his gaze, spying a rectangular box by the knife block. "Did you get a package? What is it? Why are you so upset?"

"Not me. *You.*"

"You opened her mail?" Scarlett asked, placing a mittened hand on each hip. "That's kind of illegal, right?"

"I was expecting a package from Amazon, and when I saw the smile logo, I thought it was mine. I didn't realize until I had already..." He lifted his eyes from the box and moved them over to Lauren without blinking. "You need to see this."

Lauren stepped toward Shane. If this was his reaction to the box's contents she wasn't sure she even wanted to know what was inside.

"Go on," Scarlett nudged her. "I've been hanging onto that thing for weeks. I'd love to know what's inside."

Lauren's hands shook, which was ridiculous. Why would a stupid box from back home make her so nervous? And why did Shane look as if he'd seen a ghost?

She placed a hand on the counter to steady herself, then looked inside. On top lay a folded pink afghan, which she carefully lifted up and held to her cheek.

Soft, familiar... and altogether confusing.

Next she found an old teddy bear with big, exaggerated lips, blonde hair, and a little white dress. She knew this bear. It had been hers years ago, and she'd called it *Lola*.

A folded letter lay on the bottom with two glossy photographs. The first matched one of the many photos in her memory box. It showed her as a toddler, sitting on her mother's lap. They both wore matching purple polka-dot dresses. Her mother's hair was teased high into the air, and Lauren's little curly wisps were held back with a delicate lace headband. It was the last picture she'd ever taken with her mother, which made it special to her.

But how had somebody else gotten ahold of it, and why would they go to the trouble of sending it to her?

She glanced at the return address on the box, but it was from her friend Helen in New York, who'd simply forwarded the package on to Alaska.

"Look at the other picture," Shane said gently, coming up beside her and lacing his fingers through hers. Scarlett joined her on the other side and put an arm around Lauren's shoulders. Whatever was in this box would likely change her life, but she had two great friends to help her face whatever came next.

She took a deep breath and reached for the other photo.

In it an older woman with Lauren's same wavy brown hair smiled at the camera from atop the Empire State Building. Wind whipped her hair and caused her to squint, but Lauren recognized those brown eyes. She had always bemoaned the fact that she hadn't inherited her father's intense green eyes... because she'd gotten brown ones from her mother.

From this woman.

"I don't understand," Shane said from beside her. "You told me your mother died when you were little."

Lauren gulped. "She did. At least, I thought she did."

"Read the letter," Scarlett said. "I'm sure there's a logical explanation."

Lauren dropped the photos back into the box and

covered them up with Lola the bear and the old afghan. "I can't," she whispered. It was the only way to make sure she didn't scream in that moment. "I can't handle this right now." A sob wracked through her body and both her friends wrapped her into a tight group hug.

"You don't have to until you're ready," Scarlett assured her.

"You don't have to ever," Shane corrected. "We can set it on fire. We can make it go away."

"No," Lauren mumbled into his shirt collar. "I want to know why, but I need some time before I'm ready to find out the truth."

"Should we have some stew and talk about other things?" Scarlett offered.

"Yes, please," Lauren answered with a sniff. She looked back at the box one last time before Shane moved it out of sight.

She didn't know how to feel. On the one hand, maybe it would have been better if the post office had lost this box on one of its many trips. On the other, she had a mother now. Growing up, she'd always wished her mother had been alive, and now she was—alive, aged, and reaching out to her for some reason.

Maybe once she had some dinner in her belly, she'd have the strength she needed to take the next step.

CHAPTER 36

THE THREE OF THEM HAD A QUICK AND QUIET DINNER. Nobody had much of an appetite after the shocking news they'd partially uncovered that day, which meant Briar ended up getting more than her fair share of leftovers.

"I'm going to head home," Scarlett said once they'd finished what little they could eat. "But I can come back in a heartbeat. Call, text, Snapchat me, send a smoke signal, whatever. Just know that I'm here for you, okay?"

"I know, and I love you for it." Lauren walked her friend to the door and waited as she gathered up her things.

Shane cleared his throat as the two women hugged goodbye, and together they watched through the big front window as Scarlett drove away.

"I'm sorry I opened it," Shane murmured. "I really did think it was for me."

"It's okay. I would have told you right away anyway. You're trusting me to help with your daughter. The least I can do is trust you to help with my parents." She whispered that last word. It was the only way she could even get it out.

"Parents, wow. Earlier today I was an orphan, but now I have a mom I've never met. Did you...?" She trailed off, but Shane said nothing. Instead, he wrapped her in a tight hug and waited until she was ready to say more.

"Did you read the letter?" she asked, almost hoping he had to save her from having to read it for herself.

"I didn't. I knew it wasn't right to look at those things without you. I saw the pictures because I thought that maybe the blanket was just some kind of odd packaging. You get that sometimes with secondhand sellers." He laughed softly into Lauren's hair as they embraced.

"I just can't figure it out. Did my dad know she was alive all this time? Was he ever going to tell me? Why would they hide something like this? None of it makes any sense, Shane."

"Hush. I know." He pulled away and stroked her hair, employing a calming technique similar to one she'd seen him use with the dogs. "There's one quick way to find out."

"You want me to read the letter." She knew she had to, but she felt afraid of how the unknown words could change her life.

"Only if you're ready." He hobbled off to retrieve the box from the place he'd stored it during dinner.

As Shane set it on the end table beside Lauren's chair, she asked, "Will you stay with me? I can't do this alone."

"If that's what you want, then that's what I'll do."

"Okay," Lauren said before she could change her mind, settling into the recliner she liked to think of as hers. Her knees felt weak, and she wondered if this was how Shane felt all the time.

Shane remained standing with the help of his cane. "You've got this."

She shook her head. The tears had already begun to spill.

"Lauren, look at me," he said, and didn't continue until her eyes met his. "You're the strongest person I know. You can handle whatever that letter says."

She took a deep breath and released it through pursed lips, then unfolded the letter and read it aloud.

Dear baby girl,

It's me, your mama. I bet you didn't even think you had a mama, but here's this letter, letting you know you do.

I drove up to New York yesterday. I was so excited to see you. It was going to be a surprise.

Your father said you weren't home, that you

didn't live there anymore and that I wasn't supposed to contact you out of the blue like this. He sent me away but said I could send you a letter, and he would decide later whether or not to give it to you.

I know I did many things wrong when you were little, and I deserved to have you taken away like you were. But, Lauren, I never stopped wishing things had been different, and I never stopped loving that sweet little girl I said goodbye to almost twenty-three years ago.

As much as I missed you, I stayed away out of fairness to your father, but I can't stay away from you anymore. I need to see you one more time.

I'm including my number below. Please call me. Please give me a chance. I promise to explain everything.

XOX,

Mom

Lauren refolded the letter and put it back into the box. She knew she would read it again that night—several times at least as she tried to decipher new meaning with each iteration.

"So your father kept her away?" Shane summarized, and she realized then how much this was like the situation he faced himself with Rosie. "But I thought you were close. Why would he keep her from you like that?"

"I don't know," Lauren shook her head and focused on the rhythm of her heart to steady her breathing. "I don't know, I don't know..."

Now she was like Shane on the night his shed had caught fire, staring into the abyss—chanting the same sad words over and over, unable to look away as everything she'd once known went up in flames.

With a grunt of pain, Shane knelt down beside her chair. "Lauren, breathe."

But her breaths came fast and shallow, as if her lungs were little more than burst balloons unable to hang onto the air. Her head spun even though the room remained still.

"Please, Lauren, breathe." Shane placed a hand on her back and guided her breaths, patiently waiting until the beginnings of her panic attack receded.

"The worst is over," he said, wiping a tear from her cheek. "Call her. See what she has to say. Find out the truth, just like you wanted."

"But what if the truth is worse than the lies?" she asked, hardly recognizing her own voice as she did.

"That's a risk we all have to take sometimes when things are important to us, but Lauren, you have nothing to lose and so much to gain. You have a mother!"

"But what if I...?" She choked on a sob, no longer having

the strength she needed to fully ask any of the questions that swam frantically through her head.

"No more what ifs. The question you need to ask now is *why?* Only one person has those answers, and you're holding her number right there in your hand."

"I can't do it, Shane. I'm not strong enough."

"You are. So much more than you know, you are. You are strong, and kind, and have the biggest heart of anyone I've ever met. Lauren, you deserve to be happy. You deserve everything."

Lauren felt her heart quicken again, but this time it wasn't from her panic.

Shane felt it, too. She could tell by the way his breathing hitched and his eyelids drooped.

She gave him a small, sad smile, and he closed the distance between them, leaning over the armrest of the chair, not noticing or not caring about the pain he surely felt as he moved his body closer to hers.

When his lips met hers and the stubble on his cheeks tickled her chin, Lauren closed her eyes and let the rest of the world melt away.

In that moment, there was only Shane.

Only this.

CHAPTER 37

ALMOST AS QUICKLY AS IT HAD STARTED, SHANE PULLED away from her kiss.

Lauren smiled and leaned forward for another. She hadn't had a first kiss like this for a very long time, possibly forever. And now that she'd started kissing Shane, she never wanted to stop.

He leaned back as she leaned forward, causing her to giggle. It was always a challenge with him, even when they were supposed to be in perfect sync. Shane struggled back to his feet, and she joined him.

"Don't look at me like that," he said, wrapping her in a hug.

"Like what?" As he wrapped his arms back around her, Lauren smiled so hard it hurt her cheeks.

"Like you could love me," he whispered.

"Maybe I can," she confessed, knowing that she was already most of the way there.

She tried to look up to gauge his reaction when she said that, but he pressed his lips to her forehead, his scratchy beard tickling her eyelids.

"Go call your mother. That's what's most important now." His face brooked no argument, and besides, he was right. As much as Lauren wanted to lose herself and all her problems inside of Shane's kisses, she'd come all this way to learn the truth—a truth that was now only a single phone call away.

"Will you stay with me?" she asked. "I can't do this, not alone."

"Sure." He pulled back yet again and went to settle himself in his recliner.

"Here goes nothing," Lauren said with a deep breath as she punched in the cell phone number from the bottom of the letter and waited for it to ring on the other end.

"Hello?" a woman answered with a strong, clear voice.

Lauren hadn't thought about how she would start this call, and now she felt herself faltering. No words seemed right. The situation itself didn't seem right.

"Look, if this is a prank call, I'll—"

She looked over at Shane, who nodded his encouragement, then said, "It's me, Lauren."

"*Lauren*. Oh, Lauren!" The bell-like voice quavered

now. "I thought you didn't want to see me. I thought I would... Never matter, you're calling now and I'm so, so grateful."

"I moved after Daddy died and I only just got the package tonight," she explained. "I had no idea you... He told me you'd died."

"Yes, that was the arrangement. I'm sorry about your father." Her mother sighed on the other end of the line, and Lauren wanted to reach through the phone to hug the woman who was a stranger but also wasn't.

She had so much to say, so much to ask. Only one word rose to her lips. "*Why?*"

Another sigh. "That's a long story with mistakes made on both ends. It's better that I explain in person. Where are you? When can I see you?"

Lauren shook her head as she tried to take this all in. She didn't want to wait. She'd already waited for more than twenty years. "I'm not in New York anymore. I found this box, and... Actually, that's a long story, too. I'm in Alaska, outside of a small town called Puffin Ridge."

"Alaska? What are you doing up here?"

"What do you mean *here?*"

"Alaska, of course." And for the first time in memory, Lauren heard her mother's laugh. It sounded exactly the same as her own. How many other parts of Lauren had she unknowingly inherited from this woman?

"Alaska's where I was born and raised and am now back for more."

"Oh, I had no idea."

"There's a lot you don't know yet, but I'd really like to be able to tell you. It's late tonight, but I'm just outside of Wasilla, a couple hours away. Can I come see you tomorrow?"

"I'll meet you partway," Lauren said. "Name a place and a time in the city, and I'll be there." Odd how it felt like she was arranging a business meeting and that the business in question was her life. They made plans for breakfast the next day and said goodbye.

When Lauren looked to Shane, he smiled.

"I can't believe I'm going to meet my mom tomorrow." She stood again. All the strength had returned to her limbs and now, she felt almost invincible.

Shane looked far less happy than she felt, so she fumbled for an explanation.

"I'm sorry about the dogs. I just didn't want to wait a single second longer than I had to."

He bowed his head toward her. "It's okay. I understand."

"Shane? Will you come with me?"

"If that's what you want, then I'll come. Now go get some rest. Big day tomorrow."

"What about you?"

"I'll be in bed soon myself. Just want to catch up on some reading first."

She waited for him to stand and embrace her, but he remained seated.

"Good night," she said, sweeping in to offer him a kiss on the cheek. "See you in the morning."

❄

LAUREN HAD a hard time sleeping that night. Her thoughts shifted from Shane to her mother to her father and back. As excited as she was to learn her mother was alive and to meet her the next day, one or both of her parents had done something seriously wrong to keep this from her all these years. What circumstances could possibly lead to such a lie?

She didn't want to be angry at her father, but she couldn't help it. He'd lied to her her entire life, deprived her of a mother.

And was her mother any better? She just accepted the arrangement when she should have fought harder for her little girl, fought harder for Lauren.

Then there was Shane. He'd acted strange after their kiss, but what a kiss it had been! He wouldn't have been able to kiss her like that unless he felt every bit as much for her as she did for him. Still, he'd warned her not to love him. Did that mean he already loved her? And had he insisted she call her mother because it was best for her or as a way of changing the topic?

Questions, questions—as always, Lauren's life was full of them. She finally fell asleep in the early morning hours with all these questions temporarily falling to the back of her mind.

When she awoke, she felt exhausted but cautiously optimistic about how the day might go. Besides, Shane would be there with her, which meant at the very least she would have a friend to help her get through whatever happened with her mother.

She quickly fed the dogs, then came in to take a shower and get ready. Normally, Shane was up with her in the mornings as they now worked together to care for the team. Today, however, he'd slept in late.

Had he hurt himself more than he'd let on when he knelt to the floor beside her? Or had her tossing and turning last night kept him up, too?

Although she was almost ready to leave, she still hadn't seen Shane. Growing impatient, she padded through the hall to his bedroom door. As she rose her hand to knock, she saw that he'd left a note for her.

I'm sorry.

I had other things to take care of.

Will see you tonight.

Good luck!

What could possibly be more important than this? Lauren wondered. He was building walls between them again. Maybe he hadn't meant to kiss her at all. But it was also possible that he *did* have something important to take care of. *Maybe* it was killing him not to be there for her today.

She decided to believe the latter, because the alternative was too painful—and she needed all her strength to get through this day, especially now that she'd be on her own.

CHAPTER 38

LAUREN REACHED THE BROKEN EGG DINER EARLY, BUT HER mother was earlier, waiting with two cups of coffee in a booth at the corner of the packed restaurant. There was no mistaking her. This was the woman from the picture, the woman who looked so much like an aged version of Lauren.

And apparently her mother recognized her, too. When she saw Lauren approach, she stood and wrapped her in a tight hug. "My little Lauren is not so little anymore. It's so good to see you, sweetheart!"

Lauren stiffened in her embrace. She felt so many things being here that she couldn't be sure which was strongest. Anger over having been abandoned? Joy at finally having a mother? She just didn't know.

Her mother cleared her throat and motioned for Lauren

to sit across from her in the booth. "You look so much like I did at your age. I'd recognize you anywhere, I think."

Lauren stirred some creamer and sugar into her coffee and took a sip.

Her mother frowned for a moment, but then immediately forced an overly bright smile. "I'm sorry. This must be so strange for you."

"I don't even know what to call you," Lauren admitted with a pert nod.

"How about mom? Or if you're not ready for that yet, Barb?"

Lauren shrugged. "I don't know what I'm ready for. This is all so… so much."

"I know, dear. I can't imagine what you must be feeling."

"I'm not even sure I know that myself. Could you maybe help me understand what happened?"

Barb—it was too hard to think of this stranger as mother, not until she knew the truth—let out a long sigh, something Lauren had already noticed she did a lot. "I'm afraid that part doesn't make me look too good. You have to understand it was a long time ago and I was very young, even younger than you are now."

The waitress came over and brought them each a plate of blueberry pancakes. "Need anything else, dears?" she asked, unloading rolled up utensils from her apron and a handful of butter packets.

"We're fine, thank you," Barb answered politely. When the waitress had skittered back to the kitchen, she added, "I took a chance and assumed you might love these flapjacks as much as I do."

Barb's smile was contrived. She was trying way too hard, which convinced Lauren that her big reveal would be tough on the both of them.

Lauren braced herself against the booth and said as firmly as she could, "I need to know."

The older woman sighed yet again. "I'll tell you, but please don't leave until I've told you everything."

Lauren nodded, not knowing whether she'd be able to keep such a promise but willing to try. Barb fixed her eyes on Lauren's stack of pancakes, which made her feel as if she couldn't eat them. She nursed her coffee instead as she listened to the untold tale of her past unfold.

"I met your father the summer after high school. He was older, a college boy, and I was absolutely smitten. But summer came to an end, and I'd already planned to move to LA to work as a waitress while I waited to be discovered. So we broke up and I went on my merry way. A few months later, I realized I was pregnant. I didn't want to kill it—kill you—so I figured I would give the mother thing a shot."

Lauren hadn't realized her parents had considered abortion, even briefly. It hurt to think she could have never been born at all, could have never had the chance to find out the truth now. Thank God for small miracles. As confusing as all of this was, at least she was here and able to hear it.

Barb reached for Lauren's hand, which seemed like a good time to dig into her pancakes, after all.

Sigh. "Lauren, I tried. Honest to God, I tried. But I kept missing auditions, showing up late for rehearsals, and losing parts to girls who were 'more committed.' I loved you, but I hadn't asked to be a mother. Meanwhile, show biz had been my lifelong dream, and I could feel it slipping away."

Lauren popped a bite into her mouth and did her best to focus on the flavors and textures on her tongue rather than the bitter sting in her chest. Her mom hadn't wanted her, and she had a pretty good idea of what would come next in this story. If she thought of it like a story, maybe it wouldn't hurt quite so much. She swallowed and took another bite as Barb continued.

"So I packed you up and took you to Alaska to see if I could find your father. Since he was listed on your birth certificate, I knew it would be easier for everyone if I could convince him to take you. It wasn't hard to find him. He was a big musher then, and I waited for him at the finish line, holding you bundled up in the cutest little snowsuit that made you look like an angel.

"He recognized me instantly and invited me for a meal to catch up on old times. I told him that you were his, showed him the birth certificate and everything, and he was a smart man. He did the math and understood. I explained that I couldn't take care of you anymore and that I wanted to offer him the chance before giving you up for foster care."

Foster care? It's as if her early life had ricocheted from one bad situation to another. All things considered, she'd been very lucky to have the childhood she did. And she knew that was all thanks to one person—though not the one sitting before her.

Barb voiced the words that were already in Lauren's mind. "Your father was a good man. I hope you understand that. Less than an hour before, he hadn't even known he had a daughter, and now he was agreeing to take you in, to do whatever it took to make sure you stayed out of the system.

"He said he would take you, but it wasn't a decision I could take back. Not ever. He wanted me to promise to stay away, saying it would only hurt you if you knew."

He was right, Lauren thought. *He was absolutely right. And I doubted him. I questioned whether he really loved me at all. When he loved me so much, so instantly, that he put everything aside to be there for me.* Lauren wished she could tell her father how much she appreciated the hard decisions he'd made for them both, wished she could apologize for ever questioning his motives, begrudging him his secrets.

Barb continued the story, cutting into her pancakes and beginning to eat now. Apparently, the hardest part was over

—at least for her. "I agreed, but after a couple years, I grew to regret my decision. My career never took off like I hoped it would, and I'd given you up for nothing. I came back to Alaska to find you but learned your father had moved out of state and taken you with him. He'd left everything to keep me from getting to you, like he knew I would change my mind and try to take you away again."

They both took a bite and chewed in companionable silence.

Barb swallowed and set her fork and knife down at the edge of her plate. "Back in those days, it wasn't so easy to find people. We didn't have Facebook and things like that. I searched and searched, but eventually gave up. That is, until…"

The older woman's face grew pale, and Lauren wondered whether it was due to sincere feelings or part of a performance she'd decided to put on for Lauren's benefit. Her voice shook now and her eyes glistened with the promise of tears. Lauren still didn't know whether any of it was real.

"Until the doctor found the cancer in my blood. I'd waited too long, and now nothing but prayer was going to save me. So I skipped the chemo and radiation and instead decided to make sure my business was in order before I had to come face to face with my maker. That business started with finding you and making things right in the time I had left."

Oh, shoot. Soon Lauren would be an orphan yet again. As much as she wanted to remain angry over the poor decisions her mother had made, she also couldn't deny that this woman had gone out of her way to find Lauren now. She'd been honest when she could have just as easily as maligned Lauren's father. They were here together now, and from the sounds of it, there wouldn't be too many other times like this. She reached across the table and gave her mother's hand a supportive squeeze.

Barb smiled sadly at her, the story almost through. "I hired a private detective and traced you and your father to that town in New York. I called him and asked him to come meet me to talk. Later on, I found out that he'd gotten in a crash driving home from that meeting. And I felt so guilty that I'd caused you to lose both your parents now, but I'd already sent the package, and even though I knew now I didn't deserve it, I hoped beyond hope that you'd reach out to me, maybe even forgive me, so I could have the chance to get to know you before I..."

"Stop," Lauren said softly. "You don't have to say anything more. I'm glad we found each other, and you did the best thing in the world by getting me to my dad. I've had a good life, and I can't wait to tell you all about it."

They continued to hold hands across the table for a few

minutes more. There they were together in solidarity, mother and daughter reunited at last. Lauren felt the anger melt away just like the butter on the second helping of steaming pancakes she'd requested. Finally, she would have her own memories of her mother. She had a family again, and that meant everything.

CHAPTER 39

LAUREN SPENT THE DAY CATCHING BARB UP ON ALL THE years she'd missed while Lauren had been growing up without her. She still didn't know how to feel about her mother's confession, but she now understood why her father had kept this part of his life secret.

To keep her safe and protect her heart.

Love, plain and simple. She hated that she had ever doubted her father's motives. As for her mother, she chose to forgive her. Although Barb's actions had been insanely selfish, Lauren had still lived a great life with a parent who loved her more than anything.

It rankled, knowing she could be set aside so easily for a ridiculous pipe dream, but at the same time, she knew that not forgiving her mother now would lead to a lifetime of regret later.

If Lauren stayed away while she sorted out her feelings, it could be too late. Barb was dying. She'd worked hard to find Lauren and said she was sorry for everything that had happened. The least Lauren could do now is give herself some closure, take the chance to get to know her mother, and view this turn of events as a gift rather than a burden.

She drove home late that evening, having made plans for Barb to come up to the cabin later that week for a home-cooked meal. It felt strange to have solved her father's mystery, but it also felt fated that she was here in Alaska, living in the state where her parents had met and fallen in love and following in her father's footsteps, living the dream he had abandoned to give her a good life.

She couldn't wait to tell Shane everything she had learned that day, but apparently she had to. When she reached the cabin, an unfamiliar car was parked outside—a much fancier one than she'd ever seen around Puffin Ridge.

Was this the thing that needed taken care of, per Shane's note that morning?

Something felt off.

She pushed through the door, not knowing what she would find on the other side. Briar jumped up on her and then raced around the room in excitement.

"That dog needs to learn some manners," a thin, dark-haired woman said from the recliner where Lauren normally sat. She wore knee-high boots with stiletto heels over her designer jeans, an outfit that looked ridiculous in this weather. She caught Lauren examining her and laughed. "Is this my replacement, Shane?"

Shane turned bright red beneath his beard. "This is Lauren, my handler. Lauren, this is my ex-wife, Satan."

"Oh, you always were a funny one, weren't you?" the woman said with a furrowed brow.

So this was Isabel? The woman was clearly all wrong for Shane. From her overly made up face to the tips of her designer footwear, *all wrong*.

"Can we help you with something?" Isabel asked in a syrupy sweet voice.

"I was just..." Lauren started.

"Grabbing a chair," Shane finished for her. "Here, take mine. I'll get one from the kitchen."

"There's no need for all of this, Shane," Isabel said. "I told you I'll leave as soon as you sign the papers." She reached into her bag and pulled out a manila envelope, waving it at him.

"And I told you I'm not signing anything without having my lawyer look it over first." Shane settled himself on the arm of Lauren's recliner rather than getting a third seat from the kitchen.

Isabel frowned, but her forehead remained smooth and unwrinkled. "You made me drive all this way. For what? It's like you wanted to waste my time."

"That is a perk," he said with a scowl.

Isabel placed an arm on each of the chair's rests as if it were a throne. "You're nothing, Shane. You're less than nothing. The best thing I ever did was leave you. Best thing I ever did for my daughter, too."

Lauren was not going to sit back and watch as Shane was treated like this, and in his own home, no less. "Excuse you, Rosie is Shane's daughter, too, and she deserves to have her father in her life."

"Your *handler*, you say?" Isabel raised an eyebrow at Shane, ignoring Lauren completely.

"He told you he doesn't want to sign the papers right now, so I think it's time for you to go." Lauren rubbed Shane's back, hoping it would comfort him somehow.

Isabel leaned forward, her hair falling in front of her face, making her resemble the freaky little girl from *The Ring* movie. "I don't have to listen to him, and I certainly don't have to listen to you. That's the handy thing about a divorce. If he didn't intend to sign these papers, he wouldn't have invited me over. Nobody asked you for your thoughts, and nobody cares. I can guarantee that much. Now go out with the dogs where you belong, you little bi—"

"I don't think so!" Lauren rose from her chair and stomped over to Isabel's.

Shane grabbed her wrist, but she shook him off.

"Leave the papers, and get out."

"Or what?" Isabel laughed at her.

"Remember, you had your chance," Lauren growled. She could be a beast, too, especially when it came to protecting the people she cared about—people that most definitely included Shane. She grabbed the other woman's arm and pulled her from the chair, marching back toward the front door.

"What are you—?"

"Taking out the trash."

Isabel ripped her arm out of Lauren's grasp and rubbed her thin wrist. "He can never love you, sweetie. He doesn't know how."

She stalked back to the chair to grab her purse and threw the envelope at Shane. "Nice seeing you, Shane. Maybe next time you can fight your own battles, eh? I'll be back tomorrow for my *signed* papers. You can count on that."

CHAPTER 40

When Lauren slammed the door and turned toward Shane, she found that the tremor she hadn't seen in weeks was now back. Honestly, she couldn't blame him.

"She was... *charming*," Lauren said with a huff. "Why did you let her in?"

"She said it was about Rosie. I thought maybe something had happened to her and that I could help, but then Isabel showed up and with these papers." He held up the envelope, which was still sealed shut.

"Mind if I take a look?" Lauren asked, crossing the room and coming to stand right in front of him. This whole thing was oddly reminiscent of her own surprise envelope the day before. Only then she'd been afraid, and now she was angry. Livid, actually.

He sighed and handed the file over. "Better you than me, I suppose. Whatever it is, it can't be good news."

"I wouldn't be so sure," Lauren mumbled as her eyes scanned the page. "Actually, it might be very good news."

She read some more, her lips moving as she did her best to discern the wordy legal jargon. "You said you lost custody of Rosie in the divorce. Right?"

Shane nodded, and she just barely caught the blur of motion from her peripheral vision. "Don't remind me," he moaned.

But Lauren pushed further. "How did you find out?"

"I was supposed to go to court for the final hearing, but I just couldn't bring myself to do it. I couldn't stand to see Rosie ripped away from me firsthand like that, and at the hands of that woman, no less. So I stayed home, and later that night, Isabel called and told me what had happened."

Of course she did. That woman was something else, and not something good.

"Shane, she lied to you." She handed the envelope back to Shane so he could see what was inside for himself.

"W-what?" He flipped through the pages, but the fresh tears that had sprung to his eyes seemed to make reading the words impossible at that moment.

"These papers, they're for the termination of parental rights. If you'd already lost them, she wouldn't be here insisting you sign. Did something happen recently?"

And just like that, his anger returned. Meanwhile, Lauren's had never left.

Shane bared his teeth. "She says she's getting married again, and this new schmuck wants to adopt my daughter."

"And he can't, because you're still legally Rosie's father."

"Does that mean…?"

"You could have been seeing her this whole time. Shane, you can go see her right now."

He shook his head and dropped his gaze toward the floor. "All this time?"

"All this time," she confirmed. "Do me a favor —stand up."

He looked to her with question marks in his eyes, but rose as instructed.

"Now put your arms around me, and look at me while I talk to you."

He drew closer and encircled her in an embrace. She had his full attention now.

"I understand you a lot better after meeting that crazy woman. You made a mistake, Shane, but that doesn't mean you have to keep punishing yourself forever. She was all wrong for you, but *I'm not.*"

He began to pull away, but she held tight to his shoulders. "Lauren, I can't—"

"I know why you think that. I see love has torn you up real bad, but it can also put you back together." She moved her hand to his heart, as if she could heal it with just her touch. "I'm not going anywhere. Please stop pushing me away."

He cried openly as he shook his head. "Isabel wasn't always like that. I did that to her. I pushed her away, too. I made my career more important than my family, and I—"

"You're human. You made mistakes, but you've learned from them. You shouldn't have to suffer for the rest of your life. You've learned, Shane. You've grown. You've changed."

Shane rested his chin on top of her head as he mumbled, "Why do you like me so much? I don't even like myself."

"Then I'll have to like you enough for both of us until you can catch up. Now kiss me again."

He leaned down and pressed his lips to hers. Slowly, she felt the tension leave his body, the pain leave his heart. It would take many more loving words and kind caresses to cure Shane of the damage he'd suffered, but Lauren would be there, waiting, ready.

CHAPTER 41

A FEW DAYS PASSED. ON EACH OF THEM, ISABEL CAME BY THE cabin, pounding and screaming at the door. Lauren had half a mind to set the dogs loose on her, but each time, she let herself out instead, calmly explaining that Shane would file his response shortly, and that Isabel would be the first to know when it had happened.

This was not news Isabel wanted to hear, which is probably why she continued to harass Shane through the door, day after day. And as much as she hated to see it, Lauren could tell that Shane was crumbling.

"Maybe I should just sign," he said after Isabel had paid them a visit that day.

"If you give up now, then you're just as crazy as she is. Maybe even more." Lauren plopped into his lap and looked him straight in the eye, which was especially easy considering their faces lined up perfectly in this position. "Shane, this is your daughter."

"I know. *That's* why I'm considering signing." He ran his fingers through her hair, not removing his gaze from hers for even a second. "What if Rosie actually loves this new guy? What if he'll be a good father to her, and I'm ruining that? I wasn't there for her when I had the chance, and now it's too late."

"You've got to be kidding me. Remember how my mom and I reconciled after more than twenty years apart? Good thing she's coming over tonight. She can remind you herself and tell you how stupid it would be to walk away from that relationship." Lauren gave him a quick kiss and left Shane alone to his thoughts.

Sure enough, Barb came early for dinner that night, eagerly offering to help with the prep work. "I worked as a cook for many years," she explained while expertly julienning a carrot. "The moment I was no longer pretty enough to bring in the really big tips, they moved me to the back of the house. Lucky for me, I liked it there. And so that's where I stayed until I decided it was time to move back to my home state."

"Lauren's a great cook, too," Shane said, wrapping his arms around her from behind as she washed the lettuce for their salad. "I bet you have lots of things in common and don't even realize it yet."

Lauren turned her face to the side and accepted a kiss on the cheek from Shane. "I bet it's that way with you and Rosie, too."

At hearing the little girl's name, Briar's ears perked up and she let out a low whine.

"See?" Lauren said, shaking him off and scrambling over to comfort the poor dog. "She hasn't given up yet, and neither should you."

"Giving up?" Barb asked, washing her hands and drying them on a plain white tea towel. "Do you have a daughter, Shane?"

"Her name is Rosie, and she's seven," he explained. "I haven't seen her for more than three years."

"Well, why on earth not?"

Shane looked to Lauren. "You haven't told her yet?" he asked, referring to the fact that Barb and Lauren had talked on the phone every night that week.

Lauren returned to the other side of the kitchen and poked Shane in the chest, standing on tiptoe to look more authoritative despite her small stature. "Why should I tell her your business? That's *your* job."

"She's not wrong," Barb said with a chuckle, turning on the gas over the stove and adding some butter to a cast iron skillet. "So, Shane, tell me about your daughter," she said as she shifted the melting butter to and fro to cover the entire surface of the pan.

Shane's eyes lit up as he told the women about Rose's obsession with all things pink, the way she jumped into his arms every night when he came in from working the dogs, and how her favorite bedtime story was about Clifford, the Big Red Dog. "That's how she was three years ago," he finished. "I don't know what she's like now. We only just learned that I still have partial custody."

Barb nodded along as he shared each memory. When he'd finished sharing, she said, "Now, tell me why you're willing to give up the chance to find out."

He shrugged and shrunk back from the stove. "Because I messed up. I don't deserve the chance to know her now."

"But you deserve to have your arms wrapped around *my* daughter, here in this kitchen?" Barb said with a wink.

"Trust me," Lauren said, dragging her fingers through Shane's hair. "That took a lot of convincing."

"Honey, listen to this washed up has-been. No reason out there is good enough to give up your little girl. Not a single one." The butter in the pan crackled and began to turn brown. Barb reached for the onions Lauren had chopped earlier and dumped them into the skillet.

Shane sighed and walked toward the table with the aid of his cane. "Maybe, but—"

"But nothing! If you play it stupid now, you could find yourself one day not-so-slowly dying from cancer and wondering if your girl has forgiven you enough to take a chance on meeting you."

"If you're not there," Lauren said softly. "Isabel can tell Rosie anything she wants, and Rosie will believe her, just like I believed my dad."

Barb nodded as she grabbed a hunk of ginger from the fridge. "Is that what you want? For your daughter to know you only through what someone else has to say? Or would you rather have a real relationship?"

Shane carefully lowered himself into the wooden chair. "But how?"

"Just like I did: give *her* the chance. Don't decide for your daughter whether or not she wants you in your life. She's far too young for that. Just be there. Show her it's never too late to apologize for your mistakes. Show her what a strong man looks like and what a good man does for his family."

He nodded as if suddenly the things Lauren had been telling him for days made perfect sense when explained by someone with a bit more experience on the matter. "And then?"

"Then the rest is up to her, my dear."

CHAPTER 42

WITH CONVINCING FROM BOTH LAUREN AND BARB, SHANE at last agreed that he would fight for his daughter.

Predictably, Isabel was none too pleased to hear this. "This changes nothing. Tom and I will move her to the lower forty-eight. Then you won't be able to see her anyway. I know you won't take time away from your precious dogs, and *you know* you were never cut out to be a father in the first place."

"Stay strong," Lauren reminded him each time Isabel came around. "Your daughter deserves to have at least one sane parent in her life."

Shane laughed. "Believe it or not, Isabel is actually a great mom. She's just a terrible wife, person, and everything else you can think of. It's the only reason why I was so close to giving up."

"But you won't?" Lauren said, crossing her arms. Hadn't they already been through this a million times?

"I won't," he confirmed. "Actually, I already reached out to my lawyer, and he's setting up a renewed custody hearing. He's even working on a clause that says Isabel can't move more than a couple hundred miles away from me." Shane stopped and frowned.

"That's great news," Lauren exclaimed. "So why the long face, fella?" She playfully pushed his chin to the side with her fist, but he still didn't smile.

"The date they gave us is the same day as your big race."

"So? Who cares?" she blurted.

"I care," he said, kissing her forehead. "I want to be there for your big day."

"No way are you missing that court date."

"I could reschedule for a later—"

"No, absolutely not! Shane, there will be other races, but you only have one daughter."

He continued to sulk, and it made Lauren upset with him. Could he honestly be considering undoing all the progress he'd made toward getting his daughter back over some stupid race that he wasn't even running in?

"You'll need my help to get the dogs set up, and—"

She placed a finger to his lips to quiet him. "And *nothing*. I can call Scarlett in to be my handler. She'll love that. And afterward, we can all go out to dinner to celebrate your custody decision and my big win."

Shane laughed and kissed her finger. "I love how you think. And I love you, too."

"Finally!" Lauren said with an exaggerated huff. "I was beginning to think you'd never tell me."

He looked confused. "What? That I love you? I've told you before, haven't I?"

Lauren shook her head with a smile. "Nope, that was the first time. Now if you don't mind, I'd love to hear it again."

"You're so bossy," he said, reaching down to nip her lower lip. "But it's true. I love you, Lauren Dalton."

"And I love you, too, Mr. Grump."

He pressed his forehead to hers and took in a deep breath. "You know I actually believe you when you say that," he said.

Lauren playfully hit him in the shoulder. "Hey!"

"Hey, nothing. I never quite believed Isabel. It was something in the way she said it, like there was this hesitation."

"Don't get me started on that witch," Lauren said, practically baring her teeth.

Shane continued to smile despite the unsettling change of topic. "When I win the right to custody, you'll be seeing a lot more of her. You know that, don't you?"

"I know." She shrugged it off, but his eyes remained curious as he watched and waited for her to reveal some secret truth. Frankly, the two of them had already been through enough secret truths to last a lifetime.

"Is that okay?" he asked slowly, and she rolled her eyes at him, then smiled so he would know she meant her words, every single one of them.

"Of course it's okay, because I still get you."

He brought his face close to hers and brushed his eyelids against hers. "I'm not sure why you think I'm such a catch, but I'm glad you do."

"I do. I really, really do."

Their faces remained close, and she felt each syllable caress her lips as they left his. "Then, tell me, will you still love me even if I lose?"

She nodded slightly and said, "I would love you harder, because you'd need it more."

"What if I never get better? Would you love me then?" His voice hitched on this question, and Lauren pulled back to study his face.

"That doesn't sound like a hypothetical, Shane. Is there something you need to tell me?"

His eyes seemed to quaver, as if the tremor he sometimes had in his hands had moved north. His voice came out rough, like every word had to fight to get through. "I'm not getting better, Lauren. Eventually I might be able to walk unassisted, but there's no way my knees could deal with the strain of being back behind a sled."

"But you love this!"

"I love you more," he murmured.

"Shane, no. You can have both me and the dogs. It doesn't have to be a choice."

He shook his head, and the first tear spilled onto his cheek. "It's not a choice. When they dragged me in after the accident, the doctors told me there was a fifty-fifty shot I'd ever even walk again. So far, I've been on the lucky side of that equation, figuring I could push my luck even further if I kept trying to force my body into some sort of miracle recovery. It's time I finally accepted the truth, don't you think? I'm not a musher anymore, and that's okay."

"What makes it okay that you're losing one of the things you love most in this world?" she continued to argue, losing steam as she did.

"Because I have you, Lauren."

"Some consolation prize I am."

Shane cupped her cheeks in his palms and turned her face toward his. "Lauren, you're everything I ever wanted but never dared to hope for. When the time is right and everything is settled with Isabel and Rose, I'm going to marry you, and you're going to take my place on the sled."

Lauren practically had to press the rewind button to make sure she'd heard him right. Only, regrettably, there was not remote control when it came to her life. "Wait, what? That's a lot of information to take in at once! Did you just propose to me?"

Merriment danced in his storm blue eyes. "I guess I did. Not the smoothest of proposals, huh?"

Lauren laughed. "You didn't even actually ask. I'm not sure how to answer an unasked question."

"Lauren Dalton, will you promise to love me forever? Will you take me and all that I am? Will you marry me?"

"Okay," she said with another laugh.

"That's your answer?"

She narrowed her eyes at him. Maybe she had inherited some of her mother's acting skills, after all. *"That's your proposal?"*

"I promise I'll do it right one day when you aren't expecting it," he said, lacing both of his hands through hers and rocking them back and forth over their laps.

Lauren raised an eyebrow at him. "I'd like to see that, but don't make me wait too long. It's kind of awkward living here with my boyfriend, you know. My father didn't raise me that way."

"I wish I could have met him," Shane said, kissing her eyelids.

"He would have loved you, Shane."

"I already love him for having raised such an amazing daughter. My fiancée," he said with a huge, unabashed smile.

"Look, I don't have a ring, but I will. I'll get one. Until then, I'm giving you everything else."

"What do you mean?"

"The dogs, the sled, the truck, the cabin. Everything."

"You going somewhere?"

"I'm being forced into an early retirement. My racing days are over, but Lauren, yours are just beginning."

"So?" The room started to spin. Panic. Was Shane dying, too?

But he, thankfully, put her mind at ease in the very next second. "I want you to take my place as the musher, and I want to be your handler. We'll hire someone part-time for the tasks I can't physically do. I once dreamed of being the greatest racer in the entire state, but it didn't happen for me. Together, we can make sure it happens for you. Lauren, you're incredible. You can do anything. Do you believe it?"

"I'm starting to," she said—and that was the honest truth.

CHAPTER 43

LAUREN TRIED AGAIN TO LOOK AT HER WATCH AND HER EYES met with a mound of mitten instead. Shane had to be in court right now and she wished more than ever she could be at his side, lending him her support as he faced off against the horrible witch of an ex-wife.

"Yup. That's a mitten, Lauren," Scarlett said, waving at Lauren as she hooked in another dog. "Now focus, please. We're just a couple starts away from our own."

"I was just thinking about Shane and—"

"Nope, none of that, girl. It's race time! You need to have your mind on your puppies and your puppies on your mind." Scarlett did her best to throw up mittened gang signs, and it was the most adorably awkward thing ever.

Lauren laughed as she shook out her arms and legs to

wake herself back up. "You're right, You're right. And I'm certainly lucky to have you here to keep me focused."

"That's right, you are." Scarlett laughed, patting her friend on the shoulder as she went back for another dog.

A man with a clipboard approached. "Okay, let's see here, we've got Lauren... Dalton. Is that any relation to Eddie Dalton?" the official said, marking his sheet.

Lauren nodded. "Yes. My father... He passed recently."

"I'm sorry to hear that." The official's eyes twinkled as he reached forward to shake her hand. "But you know, I used to watch him race, every chance I got. It's the reason I still volunteer at these events. I'm sure he's looking down on you right now and cheering for his little girl. And he won't be the only one."

Lauren could feel tears at the corners of her eyes. "Thank you, Mr... Um?"

"Benjamin. Ben Benjamin," he said with a friendly nod. "Yup, you won't be forgetting that one anytime soon, I'd wager."

As he looked down at the stopwatch hanging over his thick jacket, his eyes widened and he straightened his posture. "Oh, look at that, we've only got two minutes until your start, so I need to go over some stuff with you. We've blocked off the turns you shouldn't take and we've got observers at those points, just a formality. There's a flag up about a mile from the finish. We're encouraging mushers not to pass after the flag, but if you have to pass, you have to pass."

Lauren nodded numbly as the facts poured over her, and she wondered yet again if she was truly cut out for this. Scarlett patted her back and told her the team was set. She looked down the line, catching the attention of Fred and Stella by the sled, the larger dogs already tensing against their harnesses.

"Ready, Fred, Stella? Hank, Wendy, Kelly, Norm, Bob, Maude, Richard, Emily? How about you two, Jack and Carol?" she called out. The dogs yipped in response and pulled tight in their harnesses, ready to leap forward at a moment's notice.

Scarlett pulled up the snow hook and placed it on the basket before heading up to the front of the line and holding the necklines of the lead dogs. Lauren untied the tether and put her full weight on the foot brake.

Mr. Benjamin had made his way to his post and waved to her, giving her a thumbs up. She responded with a thumbs up of her own.

A sharp blast from an airhorn sounded, and Scarlett released the team in response.

Lauren hopped up off the foot brake and began running, pushing the sled like a bobsledder. "Hike! Hike! Hike!" she called out, urging the team forward.

As one, they rushed forward like a bullet from a gun, and

for one terrifying moment, Lauren thought she was about to trip and fall off the sled again. But that's not what happened. The sled picked up speed until it was out-pacing her, and she pulled against the handlebar, leaping confidently up onto the footboards.

They were moving faster than normal without Shane in the basket, but when she looked down to where he normally sat, there was a little stuffed husky staring back up at her. She laughed aloud, wishing she could call him then and there to say her thanks. Now, with the addition of her little passenger, it was as if Shane was there with her, shouting corrections and giving her advice as they went.

The sun glistened and refracted off the snow, giving the illusion of thousands of little rainbows. She looked out beyond the dogs and saw everything Alaska had to offer. There on the horizon of that beautiful landscape, she saw all the things that mattered most—her future as a musher, her future with Shane and Rosie. She even saw the smiling face of her father in the pale blue skies above her.

This was where she was meant to be. After years of not knowing her place in the world, the future now loomed clear as the whitest snow. Like the world had opened up and said, "Welcome home, Lauren."

CHAPTER 44

The race was a blur. Lauren finished fast and then left the dogs to Scarlett, not even waiting to find out her time.

"I have to get to the courthouse. I have to know how things went for Shane," she shouted excitedly as she helped Scarlett steady the sled and gave her the keys to the dog truck.

"Go, go!" her friend urged. "I'll find out your time and then pack the dogs up and get them home. Here…" Scarlett fished her own keys from her coat pocket and tossed them to Lauren. "You'll get there faster with a set of wheels. Give Shane my congratulations," she said with a mischievous smile.

"I'll give him a kiss for you, too!" Lauren shouted over her shoulder as she jogged back to the parking lot.

"Too far! Too far!" Scarlett yelled back.

And then Lauren was warming up her friend's ancient Subaru, then she was speeding through town, pulling up outside of the courthouse, running through its doors.

She looked everywhere, but couldn't find Shane. But then her phone buzzed in her pocket.

Shane!

"How'd you do?" he said the moment she picked up.

At the same time, she shouted, "Where are you?"

Both laughed.

"We're at Garcia's, out in Eagle River," he said.

"We?"

"Yeah, me and Rosie. She wanted Mexican food, and I just wanted to soak in all this wonderful Rosieness I've missed so much."

The little girl giggled in the background, and Lauren felt her heart grow two sizes just like the Grinch—or a certain Mr. Grump.

"I'll be there as fast as I can," she said, already running back to Scarlett's old station wagon.

On the way to the small suburban restaurant, Scarlett called to let Lauren know she and the dogs were about to head back to the cabin on Thornfield Way. Lauren put the call on speaker and settled the phone on her lap, since Scarlett's car didn't have Bluetooth.

"You got third, Lauren!" her friend shouted so loud that

Lauren wondered if the speaker phone was even necessary. "If this was the Olympics, you'd have a big, beautiful bronze hanging off your neck."

"That's awesome. Thank you for being there for me today, and pretty much every other day, too."

"You're worth it, kiddo. Now, tell me all about Shane. Is he over the moon?"

"Actually, he's out in Eagle River. I'm just driving there to meet him now."

"And?"

"He got his daughter back. I don't know all the details, but he's with her now. And, Scar, I have never heard that man sound so happy."

"Looks like you're going to have to find a new nickname for him now," Scar said with a laugh.

"How about Mr. Great?" Lauren said with a smile.

Scarlett let out an exasperated sigh, which quickly broke apart into giggles. "That's even worse than my jokes. Have fun and drive safe out there."

"I will. You too!"

About fifteen minutes later, Lauren floated into the restaurant, and Shane stood to greet her with a huge hug. "There's my champ!"

"More like your second runner-up," she said, "But *champ* is fine, Mr. Great." She smiled prettily at him, wondering what he would think of the new nickname.

"Mr. Great?" Shane laughed and rolled his eyes. "Did Scarlett come up with that one? That level of tacky has her name written all over it."

She rolled her eyes right back at him, then waved to Rosie, who sat with her legs tucked under her at the booth. "Hello. I'm Lauren," she said.

"Are you my Daddy's girlfriend?" Rosie asked. Lauren noted that Rosie had Isabel's dark features and delicate build, but her gorgeous blue eyes were exact replicas of Shane's.

"That's right," Lauren said. "That is, if it's okay with you."

"It's okay with me," the little girl said, scooting over in the booth and gesturing for Lauren to sit beside her. "You're really pretty, by the way." Yup, she loved this child already.

"Thank you. So are you."

"Are you going to marry my daddy like Tom is going to marry my mom?"

Lauren raised both eyebrows. "Only if you say it's okay."

Now it was Rosie who rolled her eyes. "I'm just a kid, Miss Lauren. I can't make these big decisions."

Lauren and Shane both laughed, and Rosie's cheeks turned as bright as her namesake.

The waiter came and Shane ordered a giant combo for Lauren, insisting she try a little bit of everything at Garcia's just as they had with the takeout from Maurice's.

"Rosie, I happen to know a friend of yours," Lauren told the little girl, who was coloring pictures of flowers and hearts on her placemat. She pulled out her cell phone and flicked through the camera roll. At last finding the one she wanted, she slid it over to Rosie.

"That's my dog!" Rosie cried. "Her name is Rose like me. She's Briar Rose."

"Yup," Lauren said with a smile so big it simply couldn't be contained. "It sure is, and she told me she misses you very much. Would you like to come visit her at your dad's house...?" She looked to Shane, who nodded for her to go ahead. "Maybe this weekend?"

"Oh, yes, please. I will just have to ask my mom if it's okay." Rosie bobbed her head up and down and shifted excitedly in her seat.

"That's a good idea," Shane said, reaching out to hold Lauren's hand across the table. "You should always ask your mom's permission first, but I have a sneaking suspicion that this time, she's going to say *yes*."

CHAPTER 45

One year later

LAUREN LOOKED OUT OVER THE SEA OF PEOPLE AS HER breath fogged before her on that bright March morning. She could scarcely believe that she'd made it here. She was about to run the Iditarod, and the race blogs all predicted she had a very good chance of making top ten, even though it was only her first year and even though this was the greatest race of them all.

The streets of Anchorage had been cordoned off for the ceremonial start of the race. After all the fanfare died down, it would be just her and the dogs against the great Alaskan wilderness for more than eight days at least as they made their triumphant trek toward Nome.

The familiar shape of Ben Benjamin with a clipboard

approached. "Why, if it isn't Lauren Dalton. Good to see you in the big leagues, kid. Old Eddie would be mighty proud."

"Thank you," Lauren said, "but it's Lauren Ramsey now."

"Well, lah-dee-dah! Will you look at that? A lot can change in a year. Last time I saw you, you earned third. How do you think you'll fare this time?" He drew a checkmark on his sheet as he waited for her answer.

"Honestly, Mr. Benjamin, it's not whether you win or lose. It's how you run the race."

He let out a hearty chuckle. "Are you sure you're being trained by *the* Shane Ramsey?"

Shane waved from the basket, where he sat with Rosie in front of him. "Well, I *am* her husband."

"The best husband and the best coach around," Lauren said proudly.

"Good on you, girl," Mr. Benjamin said. "You're going to go far."

"Like all the way to Nome?" Lauren's best friend Scarlett said from the back of the double sled Lauren had harnessed to her team.

"Sitting this one out, Ms. Cole?" the friendly official asked Scarlett.

"Oh, *this time*, it's just the start," Scarlett quipped. "Next time, it'll be the world." She let out her Disney villain laugh, and Rosie joined her.

"I'll just be on my way then," Mr. Benjamin said. "Good luck out there. Remember, I'm rooting for you."

They all waved goodbye and waited for the starting horn to blare.

"Got Mom?" Lauren called back to Scarlett.

"Right here in my basket," her friend answered, referring to the urn that held Barb's ashes. Lauren had spent five whole months filled with wonderful moments getting to know her mother before the cancer took her to Heaven, and she had been grateful for every single one of them.

She'd learned that it was never too late to find redemption, nor was it ever too late to discover your true heart's desire. Most of all, she'd learned how to be a mother to the beautiful eight-year-old girl who spent every weekend—and every other Wednesday—at the cabin with her, Shane, and Briar Rose.

So much had changed in the past year, and yet, Lauren felt more like herself than ever before.

The announcers called her name and off she went. The dogs wanted to perform for the crowd lining the snow covered streets. They jumped forward as one, tongues hanging haphazardly from their mouths and they raced through the city.

Along the trail, little kids were held out toward her and she gave them all high fives, a warm glow in her heart. Rosie laughed and tried to high five the spectators, too, and when she could reach, Lauren made sure to give her daughter a high five of her own.

Her daughter. Husband. Fans.

This was really her life now.

Just over a year ago, Lauren had lost her heart in New York. She'd never expected to find it here in Alaska among the new people who now made up her family, but that's exactly what had happened.

And that's how a girl who had never believed in fairy tales got her happily ever after, after all.

ARE you ready to read Scarlett's story next? This quiet librarian is about to become the main character of her own real-life adventure story...

CLICK HERE to get your copy of *The Brightest Light*, so that you can keep reading this series today!

❋

And make sure you're on Melissa's list so that you hear about all her new releases, special giveaways, and other sweet bonuses.

You can do that here: MelStorm.com/gift

WHAT'S NEXT?

Anchorage librarian Scarlett Cole has always preferred to live out her adventures within the pages of her favorite books. That all changes when she befriends junior musher Lauren, who presents her with the opportunity of a lifetime —stop reading about the Iditarod and actually get out there to race!

With her career now on the line and only one chance to establish herself amongst the dog-sledding community, Scarlett knows she'll need to work hard and with no regrets. Unfortunately, another new racer quickly sets his sights on her, vowing to triumph at any cost... even if his techniques aren't quite above board.

When Scarlett and her new rival receive a flurry of media attention, they discover that succeeding in the race could mean losing big in life. Just how much is Scarlett willing to risk to make her lifelong dream come true?

Join Scarlett, Lauren, and their courageous team of sled dogs in this unforgettable tale of dreams, destiny, and finding where you belong. Start reading THE BRIGHTEST LIGHT today!

The Brightest Light is now available.

CLICK HERE to get your copy so that you can keep reading this series today!

SNEAK PEEK OF THE BRIGHTEST LIGHT

Scarlett watched until Lauren's sled became nothing more than a pinpoint on the horizon. Her best friend had found a new life living amongst the world Scarlett longed to join for herself.

Ever since she had accepted the job as an Anchorage librarian and moved from her tiny hometown in Texas all the way north, the Iditarod had been one of Scarlett's foremost passions—along with books, of course. And now she was here, best friends with one of the top racers to watch... but watching from the sidelines.

To her, the snow glimmered with magic, the winds hinted at adventure, and helping the dogs fulfill their purpose gave her one of her own. The main problem, of course, was that dog sledding was not a sport that could be taken up casually. Her friend, Lauren, had left everything about her old life behind when she chose to become a handler for the infamous Shane Ramsey, who had since transformed into her doting husband and committed race coach.

But none of that exactly helped to bring Scarlett clarity.

Could she really starve one passion to feed another? Ultimately, racing for herself would mean quitting her job as a librarian, possibly to never return. Books were just too special for her to willingly cast aside.

She still fondly remembered herself as a five-year-old girl hanging on the arm of her papa's recliner as he taught her how to sound out the words splashed across the front page of the local *Sentinel.* She'd learned so much more than how to read—she'd learned the power of stories, the power of words.

Writing these words herself had never been on the table. She preferred to live out her adventures, either vicariously or in reality, which was what had also drawn her to the great race as she'd begun to learn about her new home state.

Now that she was also best friends with an actual musher, Scarlett's longing intensified. She'd always been happy to live between the pages, but now she craved the open air, the rushing winds, the slick drive across the snow.

Lauren was so happy, and Scarlett knew *she* could be, too. But she also didn't know how to bring this dream into actuality. Perhaps she would figure it out one day, or perhaps she would forever be stuck between two worlds, not knowing to which she truly belonged.

Her phone buzzed in her coat pocket, and she bit the thumb of her glove to pry it off her hand so she could press the teeny, tiny button to answer.

"Scarlett, you're going to have to go without me," her friend, Liz, announced without preamble.

"Without you? But we go together every year!" she argued, referring to the Miners and Trappers Ball that celebrated the start of the annual race.

"I know, I know. I'm so sorry." At least Liz did sound genuinely apologetic about the last-minute change of plans. "I would be there if I could, but something has come up."

This wasn't like her usually reliable friend, and that worried her. "Is everything okay?" Scarlett asked, fearing the worst.

"Yeah, it will be fine. I'll tell you more when I know more. I wouldn't cancel if it weren't important. You know that."

"I do, and don't worry about me. I can hang out with Shane and Rosie."

"Oh, pfffhew. Good. Okay. I'll talk to you later. Have a great time at the ball, Cinderella!"

Scarlett laughed as they hung up. She and Liz Benjamin had made fast friends almost immediately after Scarlett arrived in town. Her father, Ben Benjamin, served as one of the race officials and always had the best access to insider events, like the Miners and Trappers Ball. Liz had never much cared for racing, having grown up with it as a constant, but she was happy to help indulge Scarlett's interests.

That's what good friends did, after all. And as a good friend, Scarlett needed to feel happy for Lauren rather than envy her success.

With one last glance toward the horizon where she had last seen Lauren and the other racers charge forth toward Nome, she buried the piece of her heart that belonged to this sport and headed home to find a good book to cozy up with for the night.

Tomorrow was the ball, and she wouldn't miss it for the world.

What happens next?
Don't wait to find out...

Read the next two chapters right now in Melissa Storm's free book app.

Or head to my website to purchase your copy so that you can keep reading this sweet, heartwarming series today!

Special Collections & Boxed Sets

From light-hearted comedies to stories about finding hope in the darkest of times, these special boxed editions offer a great way to catch up or to fall in love with Melissa Storm's books for the first time.

Alaskan Hearts: Books 1-3

Alaskan Hearts: Books 4-6

The Church Dogs of Charleston: Books 1-3

The First Street Church Romances: Books 1-3

The Sweet Promise Press Collection

The Alaska Sunrise Romances: Books 1-3

The Alaska Sunrise Romances: Books 4-6

The Alaska Sunrise Romances: Books 7-9

❄

The Sunday Potluck Club

Because nothing satisfies like friendship...

Home Sweet Home

The Sunday Potluck Club

Wednesday Walks and Wags

❄

The Church Dogs of Charleston

A very special litter of Chihuahua puppies born on Christmas day is adopted by the local church and immediately set to work as tiny therapy dogs.

The Long Walk Home

The Broken Road to You

The Winding Path to Love

❄

Alaskan Hearts: Sled Dogs

Get ready to fall in love with a special pack of working and retired sled dogs, each of whom change their new owners' lives for the better.

The Loneliest Cottage

The Brightest Light

The Truest Home

The Darkest Hour

❄

Alaskan Hearts: Memory Ranch

This sprawling ranch located just outside Anchorage helps its patients regain their lives, love, and futures.

The Sweetest Memory

The Strongest Love

The Happiest Place

❄

The First Street Church Romances

Sweet and wholesome small town love stories with the community church at their center make for the perfect feel-good reads!

Love's Prayer

Love's Promise

Love's Prophet

Love's Vow

Love's Trial

❄

Sweet Promise Press

What's our Sweet Promise? It's to deliver the heartwarming, entertaining, clean, and wholesome reads you love with every single book.

Saving Sarah

Flirting with the Fashionista

❄

Stand-Alone Novels and Novellas

Whether climbing ladders in the corporate world or taking care of things at home, every woman has a story to tell.

A Mother's Love

A Colorful Life

Love & War

❄

Do you know that Melissa also writes humorous Cozy Mysteries as Molly Fitz? Click below to check them out: **www.MollyMysteries.com**

MEET THE AUTHOR

Melissa Storm is a New York Times and multiple USA Today bestselling author of Women's Fiction and Inspirational Romance.

Despite an intense, lifelong desire to tell stories for a living, Melissa was "too pragmatic" to choose English as a major in college. Instead, she obtained her master's degree in Sociology & Survey Methodology—then went straight back to slinging words a year after graduation anyway.

She loves books so much, in fact, that she married fellow author Falcon Storm. Between the two of them, there are always plenty of imaginative, awe-inspiring stories to share. Melissa and Falcon also run a number of book-related businesses together, including LitRing, Sweet Promise Press, Novel Publicity, and Your Author Engine.

When she's not reading, writing, or child-rearing, Melissa spends time relaxing at her home in the Michigan woods, where she is kept company by a seemingly unending quantity of dogs and two very demanding Maine Coon rescues. She also writes under the names of Molly Fitz and Mila Riggs.

CONNECT WITH MELISSA

You can download my free app here:
melstorm.com/app

Or sign up for my newsletter and receive an exclusive free story, *Angels in Our Lives*, along with new release alerts, themed giveaways, and uplifting messages from Melissa!
melstorm.com/gift

Or maybe you'd like to chat with other animal-loving readers as well as to learn about new books and giveaways as soon as they happen! Come join Melissa's VIP reader group on Facebook.
melstorm.com/group

ACKNOWLEDGMENTS

I have a record number of people to acknowledge for this book. Let me start with my husband, Falcon. He not only taught me about the great race, but also lent many of his own personal experiences as a handler to Lauren as part of her story.

My daughter, Phoenix, is the reason for everything, including why I write stories that are meant to uplift and inspire—as I hope this one has.

Other inspirations for this series have included my dual loves of classic literature and Disney fairytales. I decided to start the series with my favorite from each camp: *Jane Eyre* by Charlotte Brontë and Beauty and the Beast. I had lots of fun weaving in little Easter eggs, and hope you enjoyed hunting while you read!

Obviously, my five dogs were a huge source of inspiration and support for this book—especially our Pomsky girl, Sitka.

My readers, who encourage me to keep going whenever that self-doubt creeps in. Believe me, it always does, which means the books wouldn't even get written without their unwavering support and sunshine. Authors don't exist without readers, you know!

To God, for giving me the gift and the platform to tell my stories to the world.

My editor, proof-reader, assistant, colleagues, and everyone else who helped polish this book until it shined.

And my students deserve a huge thanks as well! The more than two-hundred authors who joined the course documenting the creation and promotion of this book cheered me on every step of the way. They kept me accountable, kept me on my toes and—more than anything—they taught me, too! I've loved getting to know all of them, but feel my teacher's pet, Ines Johnson, deserves special recognition. If you like urban fantasy books, then check out hers.

Thank you for taking this journey with me and enabling me to live my best life by doing what I love.

Thank you for allowing me to exist. I like being here very much, and I can't wait to see you next time in book two of the Sled Dog series.

Made in the USA
Coppell, TX
23 February 2021